Good Fortunes

A CLAIRE ROLLINS MYSTERY

BOOK 1

J.A. WHITING

Formatting by Signifer Book Design

Proofreading by Donna Rich

To hear about new books and book sales, please sign up for my mailing list at: www.jawhitingbooks.com

For all the brave people who stand up to evil

CHAPTER 1

The summer sun rose over the Atlantic Ocean promising to add another day of high temperature and humidity to the week-long heatwave that held Boston in its grip. Walking down the brick walkways to her job at the small chocolate shop and café at the edge of the North End, Claire Rollins could feel the sweat gathering on her back as she looked out at the boats docked in the harbor. The morning sun sparkled over the bright blue ocean and Claire had a powerful urge to dive into the cool sea for a refreshing swim.

Nicole, the owner of the store, was already bustling around behind the counter when Claire opened the door and stepped into the lovely air-conditioned coolness of the chocolate shop. The thirty-year-old, petite brunette smiled brightly at her employee. The two young women had hit it off immediately and had become fast friends.

"Another hot one." Claire pulled her shoulder-length blond curls up into a high bun, went to wash her hands, and then slipped the navy blue apron over her head and set to work.

"No way you're going to be able to run outside today." Nicole checked the thermostat on the wall to be sure the café would be comfortable when the first customers began to arrive.

"I know." Claire groaned. She was training to compete in a mini-triathlon in the fall and the hot summer was interfering with the goals she'd hoped to accomplish. "I'll be on the treadmill again this evening."

"When it's this hot, I bet you wish you were back on Nantucket." Nicole chuckled. "And I wish I was there with you, resting on the white sand, floating in the ocean ... aahhh."

Claire smiled. She'd spent a lot of time on the beautiful island of Nantucket, Massachusetts, but left to make a change and start over after her husband passed away. Claire's husband had been an important and well-known businessman and they'd split their time between their homes in New York City and Nantucket. After Teddy passed away, Claire sold their houses and decided to move to Boston, a place she'd loved while attending law school in the area over ten years ago. Change was in order, including a different career, but Claire didn't yet know what that would be, so as an accomplished amateur baker, she answered the ad to work at the chocolate shop until she decided on which path to the future she would place her feet.

The women chatted as they went through the morning tasks and routines preparing the coffee machines, heating hot water, carrying platters of pastries and chocolates to the glass cases, and placing trays of muffins into the commercial ovens in the back room. The chocolate shop had started out offering chocolate items in every shape and form, cookies, truffles, muffins, slices of cakes, and candies and Nicole still concentrated her business on those items, but she'd recently started carrying different flavors of pastries and candies in order to serve the customers who didn't care for or had allergies or other issues related to chocolate.

Nicole's café had been open for almost two years and it had shining wood floors, cream-colored walls, and a red-brick accent wall on one side. The place had high ceilings and huge glass windows that looked out over the neighborhood's bustling brick sidewalks, and artwork done by area artists hung on the side walls. The lighting was soft and inviting and encouraged people to gather at the wooden tables to chat, work at laptops, and enjoy refreshments.

"Are we still on for tonight?" Nicole called from the back work room.

"You bet. I'm looking forward to not having to cook tonight." Claire and Nicole planned to have dinner by the waterfront and then meet some friends for a drink at a popular bar in Boston's Back Bay. A funny sensation that Claire couldn't name ran though her body when she thought of going out that evening with Nicole. *Was it a feeling of worry? Why?* Claire pushed the idea of out her head and took a marble cheesecake from the cooler to slice into sections.

"Those cheesecakes you made came out great." Nicole nodded at the one Claire was slicing as she walked by carrying a stack of small white plates. Nicole had been teaching Claire some baking techniques and sharing recipes with her and was impressed at the way her new employee and friend was picking up everything so fast and so well. "You're a natural-born baker."

Claire smiled at the compliment. The truth was that Claire had always loved working with her hands to create things. Her mother had taught her to bake, cook, and garden, and to sew and crochet, partially because they were so poor and couldn't go out to eat or buy new clothes very often, but it was also because Claire's mom loved being self-sufficient. Claire's mother even knew some things about car engines and home electrical and plumbing systems and could manage minor and some not-so-minor repairs on her own.

The shop began to fill with the early morning regular customers and just as the line in front of the counter was growing, a third employee came in and set to work. Some customers got take-out drinks and pastries, but more people than usual chose to sit at the tables and counters to sip their morning coffees and Claire suspected that they wanted to stay inside a little longer to enjoy the cool air.

After two hours of non-stop customers, a lull descended and the women hurried around cleaning off tables and restocking the cases. Claire carried an iced coffee drink to an older woman who sat at a table in front of the sunny window watching people hurry past clutching briefcases and tourists strolling along holding guidebooks and maps.

"Here you are." Claire placed a napkin on the table and set the woman's beverage down with the ice clinking against the side of the tall glass.

The fifty-something, dark-haired woman, dressed in a long, colorful sleeveless dress, smiled up at Claire and thanked her.

Every now and then over the next hour, Claire would catch the woman sitting by the window staring at her and when Claire made eye contact, she would immediately shift her gaze to her laptop screen.

"Do you know that woman over there?" Claire whispered to Nicole.

"I've never seen her." Nicole poured iced tea into a take-out cup and snapped on the lid.

When Claire carried a tray with drinks and slices of cake to one of the tables in the corner, the woman near the windows caught Claire's eye and requested a piece of cheesecake.

"Have you lived in Boston long?" the woman asked when Claire returned with the cake.

"Just over a year." Claire wiped her fingers on the cloth she'd folded over her apron strap. "But I lived in Cambridge when I went to graduate school a number of years ago."

"I live in Cambridge." The woman smiled. "I often work from home. I have a meeting nearby in an hour so I decided to come into town early. I've never tried this café and was intrigued." After taking another bite of the dessert, the woman looked up with warm eyes. "You made this? It's delicious. You have a knack."

Claire and the woman discussed baking, Boston and Cambridge, the weather, and local news. Nicole walked by and stopped to join in the conversation and ended up telling the woman how she got involved in opening the business, her love of baking and all things chocolate, and how well the café was doing.

Nicole noticed some cards tucked under a few of the folders that the woman had placed on the table. "Oh, are those Tarot cards?"

"I dabble in using the cards." The woman moved a folder to the side and slipped some of the colorful cards out to the middle of her small table.

Claire's eyes went wide. "Tarot cards? Can the

cards tell the future?"

An easy smile spread over the woman's lips. "No. Lots of people think such things about the cards, but they can't predict the future. The cards are used to help a person connect with his or her higher self. The cards came into existence around the middle of the 1400s and were originally used for playing games. Around the middle of the 1500s, the cards began to be used for divination."

"Do you do readings?" Nicole's brown eyes looked hopeful.

"I do." The woman nodded. "Of course, here isn't the place for a proper reading, but if you'd like to come to my office in Cambridge, I can give you my business card."

"I'd love that." Nicole eagerly took the card and put it in the pocket of her apron.

The woman looked at Claire, picked up the stack of cards, and shuffled. "I'll give you a little demonstration." Spreading them over the table top, she gestured for Claire to pick up some of them. "Choose five and turn them over."

Claire didn't know why, but her heart was pounding and a strong sense of nervousness washed over her. She hesitated. "Oh, I don't know...."

"Go ahead." Nicole nudged her friend. "The cards won't tell you anything bad." She glanced at the woman for confirmation. "Will they?"

The woman smiled. "No need to worry."

Claire's forehead creased as she gingerly reached down to slide five cards from deck.

"Turn them over." The woman waited.

With shaking fingers, Claire slowly turned each of the cards to show the front pictures.

"Ah." The woman looked at the card with an image of a tower on it. "You might be searching for an easy solution to a problem you feel you have. What you sense as upheaval in your life can bring about positive change and a chance for a new beginning."

Claire's eyes widened in surprise at the accuracy of what the woman told her. The next card showed a picture of a chariot. "You are worried that things in your life are more frustrating and more of a struggle than you expected. You have the strength to manage this time of movement and change and you will emerge victorious."

Nicole smiled and nodded at Claire.

The woman glanced down to the next card, The Lovers. "You are going through a period of profound loneliness and you are suffering in silence."

Claire swallowed hard as her eyes misted over thinking of Teddy and how strongly she felt his loss.

The woman lifted her eyes to Claire and her face showed an expression of concern. "You have difficult decisions ahead, but you have the courage to handle what comes your way. It may not be easy, but you will discover happiness."

Claire knew that she had to make many decisions about her life, but she just wasn't ready to make any choices right now. She hoped that the woman was right and that her future would hold happiness and purpose.

Placing her finger on the last card, the woman slid a picture of an angry moon closer to Claire. "You are confused and fearful. Your anxieties will try to hold you back. Do not allow them to do that. You are on the right path. Things will turn out well in the end."

The woman glanced at her watch. "Oh, I must be going." She reached to gather up her cards and when Claire moved to help her, their hands briefly brushed against each other. Claire felt a spark against her skin almost like the shock from static electricity and she instinctively moved her hand back. To cover the surprise of the odd sensation, Claire reached to remove the plate and glass that were on the table.

"That was great." With a wide smile, Nicole thanked the woman for the tarot card demonstration. "I'll email you to set up a time for a reading." She headed back to the counter to wait on a customer who had just walked in.

Feeling a strange combination of unease and interest in what the woman had just done, Claire forced a smile. "Thank you. I've never seen anyone do something like that."

The woman stood up and started for the door of the café, but then stopped, turned around, and spoke in almost a whisper. "You have very strong intuition." Her face looked serious. "Do not ignore it, that intuition of yours. Be aware. Do what it tells you to do. My name is Tessa Wilcox. Contact me if you ever feel the need." She hurried out of the door with her colorful dress billowing about her ankles as she walked.

With the words of advice not to ignore her intuition ringing in her head, Claire looked through the shop window with a hard, cold fist of anxiety gripping her stomach as she watched the woman hurry away down the sidewalk.

CHAPTER 2

After work, Claire worked out in the gym just a few blocks from her apartment. She ran five miles on the treadmill and then used the stationary bike and rode fifteen miles. Even though the gym had the air conditioning on, Claire was drenched with sweat by the time she finished her workout and headed home for a shower.

Tucked at the edge of Beacon Hill was a small neighborhood of historic brownstone townhouses known as Adamsburg Square that had cobblestone streets and brick walkways that were lit up in the evenings by old-fashioned streetlamps. Some of the buildings were single-family homes while others had been renovated into two or three condo apartments and whenever one of them came on the market, the place was snatched up immediately. By a stroke of good fortune, Claire was the first to see one of the condo apartments when it became available and she swooped in and signed the lease within twenty minutes of stepping though the door.

Unlocking the glossy black door with the bronze knocker, Claire entered her apartment and dropped her gym bag on the entryway floor. The hallway led to a large living room with three enormous windows and a sliding glass door that opened to a small garden and an area of grass and shade trees that were enclosed by a high white fence.

An arched opening on the right of the living room led to a good-sized dining room with sliding glass doors to the garden. Off of the entry hall, there was a beautiful kitchen with granite countertops, high-end cabinetry, and stainless steel appliances. A door in the hall led to a small private basement with a storage area and a laundry room and a door that led out to the side alley. Two bedrooms on the left of the hallway completed the space.

When Nicole heard where Claire lived and saw the apartment for the first time, her jaw dropped. "How on earth can you afford to live here?"

Claire told Nicole that she had saved diligently when she'd worked as a lawyer, that Teddy had a good life insurance policy, and that she'd made a nice amount of money on the sale of their Nantucket home. Even though all of that was true, Claire couldn't be one-hundred percent honest about her financial situation because she was well-aware that if people knew her net worth, she could never be sure if a person liked her for her, or for her money.

After marrying Teddy, Claire was flung into the social whirl of the super-rich. The expectations and demands of being married to one of the wealthiest men in the country took a toll on her as she tried to navigate the unfamiliar waters of her new life, unsure of who could be trusted, wondering who was a real friend, and having to handle the criticisms and accusations that she was only a conniving gold-digger.

The scratch of small feet on the wood floor could be heard as two happy-faced Corgis dashed from one of the bedrooms into the living room to greet Claire. Chuckling, she bent to scratch the wiggling dogs behind their ears. "Were you asleep, Bear? How about you, Lady? What if I was a robber? You two are supposed to be guarding the apartment."

The dogs let out woofs as they followed Claire into the master bedroom. She changed out of her soaking wet gym clothes, showered, went to the kitchen and ate a snack, and then took an hour nap with the Corgis snuggled next to her on the bed. Before falling asleep, a nagging sense of unease picked at her.

***

Choosing a pale blue summer dress, beige sandals, and a blue headband to keep her soft wavy curls off her face, Claire grabbed her wallet and the small canister of pepper spray from the kitchen island drawer. Ever since she was in college, she tried to remember to carry the spray whenever she went out at night or went for a jog alone. Before heading out to meet Nicole for dinner down by the waterfront, Claire checked to be sure that the doggy door was unlocked so Bear and Lady could come and go from the house to the yard as they pleased and then she bent to pat her sweet animals. "Tomorrow we'll go to the park and you can play with the other dogs for as long as you want."

It only took fifteen minutes to walk down to meet Nicole who stood at the corner of State Street and Atlantic Avenue wearing a yellow sleeveless dress with her dark brown hair pulled up into a high ponytail. When she spotted Claire heading along the sidewalk, Nicole smiled and waved.

"You look nice." Nicole gave her friend a hug.

"You, too." Claire nodded. "It's cooler now. There's less humidity."

Chatting away and looking at the boats moored at the docks, the two strolled along Long Wharf to the restaurant they'd chosen and were lucky to be seated right away at a small table by the windows.

"Wasn't that woman with the tarot cards interesting today?" Nicole looked over the menu. "I know it's silly, but I love that stuff ... psychics, tarot cards, anything like that. I think it's fun.

Have you ever been to a psychic?"

Claire blinked and shook her head. "Never. Have you?"

"Yeah, it was so interesting. The person told me all these things about myself, where I'd traveled, things I enjoyed, people I was close to who had passed away." Nicole shook her head. "I don't understand any of it or how it might be possible, but this person blew me away. You should go to one sometime."

"Maybe." Claire didn't know why, but talking about the paranormal made her feel uncomfortable and she maneuvered the conversation away from the topic by asking Nicole questions about her life.

"My longtime boyfriend and I broke up about a year ago, just before you started working at the shop. I'd been working so hard getting the business going and he didn't like the time it took away from him. I wasn't expecting it at all." Nicole's face looked sad. "I thought things were fine between us. He hid his dissatisfaction well. I got broadsided." Looking across the table at Claire, Nicole said softly, "My loss is nothing like what you've been through."

Claire made eye contact with her friend. "Every loss is difficult." She reached over and gave Nicole's hand a squeeze and when their skin touched, a jolt of fear hit Claire so hard that she almost flung herself back against her chair. Nicole didn't notice her friend's flash of anxiety because the waiter approached the table just as it happened. After taking the young women's orders, he nodded and walked away.

Nicole smiled. "We need to talk about fun things or we're going to leave dinner completely bummed out." She started to talk about planning a short vacation once the fall came and their conversation turned to places they'd each like to visit one day and favorite vacations they'd taken.

After finishing their meals, the girls left the restaurant and decided that since the night air had cooled, it would be pleasant to walk over to Boylston Street where they'd planned to meet a few friends. Walking side-by-side through the Fanueil Hall Marketplace, the two young women passed stores and restaurants and bars and they people-watched and peeked in store windows as they strolled through the historic cobble- stoned promenade.

The first part of the marketplace had been built in 1742 and served as the market area for merchants, fishermen, and sellers of food products. Many famous speakers had addressed crowds in the marketplace or inside Faneuil Hall including George Washington, Sam Adams, and Susan B. Anthony.

Claire always enjoyed the musicians, jugglers, dancers, and other performers who set up their acts around the marketplace, but tonight she felt differently. She wondered if the string of hot and humid days was making her feel ill or if she was coming down with something. Her head pounded, her heart raced, and she felt slightly dizzy. Her unexpected discomfort made her wish she had declined the invitation to meet Nicole's friends for drinks.

Nicole chattered away beside Claire and every time Claire bumped against her friend or looked at Nicole's face, it was like a light bulb was flashing in her head. Claire had never had one, but she wondered if this was how a migraine started.

As the two headed up the street that led to the side of the Old South Meeting House, Claire broke out in a sweat, but her hands felt ice-cold. Standing at the corner waiting to cross the street, Nicole said something that Claire couldn't hear and when she turned to look at her friend, terrible images popped into her mind of Nicole laying on the sidewalk, bleeding from the chest.

Claire's ears buzzed and the words the tarot card woman had said to her clanged inside of her head. Staring at Nicole, Claire imagined seeing a ring of fire blazing around Nicole's face. As a flood of adrenaline raced through Claire's body causing her heart to beat so fast and hard that she was sure it would burst from her chest, a sense of dread hit her like a four-wheeler and nearly knocked her to her knees.

"Nic!" Claire lunged for Nicole and the two crashed to the sidewalk just as a black sedan tore up the street with a dark figure leaning out of the back window, his hand holding something that flashed hot red. Bullets flew in the girls' direction and they would have hit Nicole if she and Claire hadn't thudded to the concrete.

People's high-pitched screams filled the air as men and women darted in every direction.

Blinking, Nicole pushed herself up to sitting position and rubbed at her pulsing shoulder, pain shooting down her arm from smashing into the ground.

"Are you okay?" Claire's eyes raced over her friend looking for an injury.

"Yeah. You?" Nicole rubbed the back of her neck. "What on earth?"

A police car, its blue light flashing, screeched to a halt in front of the sidewalk where the girls had fallen and two officers jumped from the vehicle, their hands on their weapons as they surveyed the area.

Nicole shook her head and her eyes looked misty from the shock of what had just happened. "You spotted the car coming towards us? Thank heavens. If you hadn't seen it, I don't think we'd be sitting upright."

Claire stood up onto wobbly legs and reached

under her friend's arm to help tug her to her feet. She hadn't seen the car at all. She didn't even notice any traffic coming up the street towards them. All she knew was that danger was nearly upon them and that she had to act in order to save Nicole. Claire's head was pounding and she felt dizzy and unsteady.

What just happened? How did I know something bad could happen? Do not ignore your intuition. *That's what the woman in the café said to me.*

Claire's trembling fingers pushed a strand of hair out of her eyes. *But how did I know?*

CHAPTER 3

Robby, Nicole's employee, stood behind the counter filling the cases with the day's sweets, breads, and buns. "Did you hear the news about shots being fired from a car near the Old South Meeting House last night? The cops didn't catch the guy. It wasn't even that late when it happened. I walk around there all the time. It's always been a safe area."

When neither of the young women answered, twenty-one-year-old Robby, his sandy hair falling over his forehead, looked up to see their two faces staring at him from across the shop. "What? Why are you looking at me like that? I'm not making this up."

"We know." Nicole pushed the sleeve of her shirt up to reveal a huge black and blue mark running up the length of her arm. "My shoulder looks even worse."

Robby looked blankly at Nicole.

"We were there." Claire frowned and stepped around the table, pointing at her scraped and bruised knees sticking out from under her black skirt.

"No way." Robby's blue eyes were as wide as saucers as he hurried out from behind the serving counter to inspect the girls' injuries. "You were there?" His hand flew up and covered his mouth. "What happened? What did you see?" He tilted his head to better see Nicole's banged-up arm. "How did this happen? Did you get knocked down by people running away?"

Nicole shook her head. "We were standing on the sidewalk waiting to cross the street. Claire sensed something was wrong. She tackled me and we fell to the ground just as the car raced by."

Robby spun his head around to look at Claire. "How did you know something was wrong? Did you see the gun?"

Claire had no idea how she knew something was wrong, but she didn't think Robby would believe her if she told him that, so she tried to think of something to explain her feeling that danger was close to them.

A man spoke from near the door. "I'd like to ask the same thing."

The three café workers turned to see who had come into the chocolate shop. A tall man with dark brown hair and brown eyes wearing gray slacks and a navy blazer walked towards them. "I'm Detective Ian Fuller." He glanced down at the small leather notebook in his hand. "I'd like to speak to Claire Rollins and Nicole Summers." He looked at the two women standing in front of him with worried expressions on their faces and he reassured them. "It's just a follow-up to last night's interview with the police officers."

Nicole and Claire glanced at one another before Nicole took a step forward.

"I'm Nicole, the shop owner. Why don't you speak with Claire first. I'm just getting some chocolates prepared before we open for the day."

Detective Fuller gave Nicole a nod and turned to Claire. The man's gaze sent a flutter over Claire's skin that surprised her so much that she almost blushed. She gestured to a table near the windows to divert his attention from the glowing pink tinge on her cheeks.

Robby noticed Claire's fluster, raised an eyebrow, and gave her a teasing look which Claire promptly ignored.

When she and the detective were sitting at the table across from each other, the man began his interview. "Can you describe the evening for me?"

Claire recounted her and Nicole's last night's activities, from meeting and walking to the restaurant, having dinner, and then heading towards Boylston Street to meet some people for a drink. Reliving the event caused a tidal wave of anxiety to nearly choke her and she had to stop her story at the part where she and Nicole were waiting to cross the street.

"Was there a lot of traffic on the street?" Detective Fuller had his notebook flipped open and a silver pen in his hand.

Swallowing to try to ease the tension in her throat, Claire managed to squeak out her reply. "I don't remember."

"Why hadn't you crossed the street yet?"

Claire scrunched up her forehead trying to recall the details. "We were waiting for the crosswalk sign to show the green *Walk* signal."

"You grabbed your friend and hit the sidewalk, is that correct?" Detective Fuller made eye contact with Claire.

Claire nodded. She knew what he would ask next.

"What made you do that? What indicated the need to duck?"

The corners of Claire's lips turned down and she gave a shrug. "I really don't know. Something seemed off, but I didn't know what it was or why I felt that way." She hesitated for a moment and then said, "Maybe it was intuition."

The detective held her eyes. "Think back on the night. Imagine yourself standing at the corner. What did you hear? Describe what you saw."

Claire turned her head and, through the window, watched the activity on the street outside the shop.

A wave of sickness rose from her stomach into her throat as she imagined herself and Nicole standing on the corner in the dark. Clutching her hands together in her lap, Claire leaned back against the chair and sucked in a few deep breaths. She lifted one hand and passed it over her eyes, as she murmured, "Sorry."

"It's okay." The detective leaned forward and his voice was calm and reassuring. "Feelings bubble up. You don't expect the intensity of them. It's the body's way of trying to protect us. Time passes ... and those intense feelings will fade gradually."

Feeling light-headed, Claire gave a slight nod, but squeezed her hands together even harder, determined not to give in to the sensation of vulnerability that washed over her when she thought back on what happened the previous night. The detective's kind words lessened the racing of her heart and she attempted to go on with her story. "Nicole and I were waiting for the light to change so we could cross. In a split second ... no, it was less than a split-second, I felt a terrible sense of impending doom so I grabbed Nic and pulled her down to the sidewalk." Claire rubbed her forehead. "If I'd stopped to think about what I felt compelled to do, I would have held back, thinking how stupid it all was."

"Instinctive feeling has protected human beings for thousands of years." Detective Fuller held

Claire's eyes. "It's the ability to know that something is likely without conscious reasoning playing a part. It's like a sixth sense that tries to guide us. More people should listen to their instincts."

Narrowing her eyes, Claire gave the detective a slight look of skepticism.

"It's true." Detective Fuller nodded. "In interviews with victims of crimes, time and time again, the person reports having feelings of unease or a sense that they should get out of the situation, but then they dismiss their feelings as foolishness because the reasoning mind tells them that nothing is amiss. That sixth sense is on alert and is trying to warn the person that something is wrong and everything is *not* fine." The detective paused. "It's good that you listened to the warning."

Claire relaxed slightly, thankful that Detective Fuller did not make light of her reaction to something she didn't understand. "All I can recall is the feeling of alarm. I don't remember anything about our surroundings that seemed odd or off." She gave a shrug, sorry that she couldn't be of more help. "We were on the ground when the gun fired from the car. I only heard the shots. I really couldn't tell the make or model of the car. It all happened so fast. I'm not even sure that I could tell you with any certainty that it was a *dark* vehicle." Claire tried to lighten the mood. "Next time, I'll try harder."

Detective Fuller smiled at her. "Let's hope there isn't a next time."

Claire admired the man's high cheekbones and the strong cut of his jaw and marveled at the way the detective gave off a combination of authority mixed with a kind, gentle manner. What Detective Fuller asked next yanked Claire out of her idle thoughts and back to the reality of last evening's mess.

"Is there anyone in your life, or who you know, who would wish you harm?"

The question hit her like a ton of bricks and Claire's jaw dropped, not because there was anyone she thought of who wished her ill, but because the possibility chilled her that there could be someone who wanted to harm her.

"Is there anyone who would want you dead?"

The detective's question made Claire's heart race. Trying hard to keep her voice even, she shook her head. "No."

Reaching into his pocket, the detective retrieved a black leather business card holder and slipped one of the cards from inside. He slid it over the tabletop to Claire. "If you think of anything else, give me a call."

Picking up the card with shaky fingers, Claire stood. "Thank you."

Detective Fuller held Claire's eyes. "Call me

anytime at all."

A feeling of warmth rushed through Claire's body. "I'll have Nicole come over to talk to you now." Walking away to retrieve Nicole from the back workroom, her legs felt weak and wobbly and her heart was pounding, but Claire didn't think it was solely due to recalling the gunshots from last night.

Grinning, Robby raised an eyebrow and leaned close to Claire as she passed him. "I think Mr. Detective has his eye on you ... and not because you're guilty of anything."

Heading into the back room, Claire shot a few daggers out of her eyes at Robby and ignored his comment, but she realized with surprise that she almost wished that it was true.

CHAPTER 4

As soon as the first customers started to file into the café, Nicole and Detective Fuller ended their conversation and Nicole, looking white as a sheet, hurried to the serving counter to wait on some of the regulars. Claire watched the detective leave the chocolate shop with a slight twinge of regret. She leaned towards Nicole as the young woman brushed past to go behind the counter. "Are you okay?"

"I guess so." Nicole's facial muscles looked tense. "Let's talk after the morning rush."

It was nearly noon when things finally slowed down and they got the chance to properly refill the cases, wipe down the café tables, and carry trays of dirty dishes to the back room to load into the dishwashers.

"Where did all those people come from?" Robby opened the chocolate case and added new sweets to the trays. "Did a bunch of tour buses park out front and dump people at our door?"

Claire chuckled, one of her blond curls had

slipped from her ponytail and bobbed next to her temple. “The chocolate shop must have been added to a list of favorite places to see in Boston.”

Nicole stepped from the back room looking frazzled. “I’ll be working all night to replenish what we sold today.” Pushing a stray lock of her hair back from her face, she smiled. “I’m not complaining though, really I’m not.”

Robby glanced at Claire. “She *is* complaining.”

“Maybe a little.” Nicole’s shoulders sagged a bit as she washed out the containers that were used to make frozen coffee drinks and admitted, “I’m exhausted.”

“I’m sure you slept as well as I did last night.” Claire frowned and turned to Robby. “We got home late after speaking with the police and I just could not fall asleep. The whole thing kept replaying in my mind. I kept hearing the gunshots.”

Nicole leaned back against the counter with her arms crossed over her chest. “Detective Fuller asked me if there was someone who might want me dead.”

“He asked me the same thing.” Claire tried to push the worry from her mind that there might be someone who wanted to hurt her, but her thoughts raced as she thought back to when her husband died. Teddy Rollins had never been married before he exchanged vows with Claire at the age of seventy-three years old. Though, he’d never had children and he had no siblings or cousins and his parents were long dead, none of that stopped people from coming forward after Teddy's death with claims to the man's fortune. In the midst of her grief, Claire had to retain several attorneys to field and handle the avalanche of demands and assertions of people who were determined to get their hands on the money.

Several of Teddy's supposed friends and a good number of his higher-up employees and business associates maneuvered to takeover the companies and holdings and many made scathing and almost threatening comments to Claire to intimidate her to back down. Overwhelmed and exhausted, Claire nearly did give in, but when she told her lawyers to stop fighting the claims, they held lengthy discussions with her and advised her to hold on and honor the wishes of her late husband who wanted Claire at the helm of all he'd accomplished.

A cold finger of fear traced down Claire's back as she pondered the possibility that someone from Teddy's past might be targeting her and that one of those past business associates might be behind last night's gunshots.

"He asked you that? The detective asked you if someone might be trying to kill you?" A look of horror washed over Robby's face as he turned, wide-eyed, from Claire to Nicole. "*Is* there someone who wants you dead?"

"That question ... it unnerved me." Nicole shuddered slightly. "Almost more than getting shot at."

Claire rubbed her arms. "I got so light-headed when Detective Fuller asked me if someone I knew might be trying to kill me that I was afraid I was going to pass out right there in the chair."

Robby asked again, a bit of panic at the edges of his tone, "*Is* there someone who wants you dead?" He glanced to the front door as if he wanted to rush over and lock it.

Even though both young women couldn't be sure if someone was out to harm them or not, they looked at Robby at the same time and answered in unison, "No."

An audible sigh of relief escaped Robby's throat just as a flash of lightning lit up the room and a booming crack of thunder shook the building. The few customers sitting near the windows almost jumped from their seats from the sudden thunderbolt and just as suddenly, rain poured from the sky and pelted the glass.

A young woman with long black hair burst through the door of the chocolate shop dripping wet. Pushing her damp hair back from her face with both hands, she reached for some napkins from one of the tables to wipe the drops of rain from her arms.

Claire hurried over with two clean dish towels.

"Here, use these. They'll work better than napkins."

"Thanks." The woman rubbed the towels against her arms and legs and then used them to press the dampness from the ends of her hair. Shaking her head and giving Claire a smile she said, "A minute ago it was sunny."

Claire shrugged. "You know the saying ... if you don't like New England weather...."

With a chuckle, the dark-haired woman finished the sentence. "Then wait a minute."

Taking the dish towels from the woman's hands, Claire noticed a white gauze bandage wrapped around her upper arm. "Would you like something to drink?"

"I would, but I'd also like to talk to you ... and the other woman who works here."

Claire stood frozen for a few moments staring into the dark brown eyes of the young woman standing before her. She had the feeling that the conversation they were about to have would plunge them all into something that made her stomach clench like a tight fist. "Okay, sure. Have a seat. I'll get Nicole."

Hurrying to the back room, Claire noticed that the woman chose a table away from the other patrons. Robby scurried behind Claire and was about to follow her into the prep area. "What does the mystery woman want?"

Claire said, "I don't know. Yet. Would you go and take her order?"

A worried look washed over Nicole's face when Claire came to fetch her and it was still there when they settled in chairs at the woman's table.

"I'm Merritt Handley." The woman introduced herself as she set down her latte cup. Claire estimated that the young woman was about thirty years old and her posture and manner implied intelligence and good manners. She was dressed in a white, starched, sleeveless shirt and a navy blue fitted skirt, her glossy hair framed her flawless skin, and her makeup was subtle yet expertly done. "I know you don't recognize me because it's always so busy here, but I've been in a few mornings to get take-out. I work nearby in the financial district."

Nicole and Claire introduced themselves, both puzzling over what Merritt might want to speak with them about. While Nicole wondered if the woman might want to hire them to provide desserts for some upcoming company function, Claire's sixth sense was buzzing and alert.

"I want to thank you." Merritt's words surprised Claire and Nicole and they both stared at her. "I was on the sidewalk near the Old South Meeting House last night."

Claire's eyes widened and she glanced quickly at the bandage on Merritt's arm.

Merritt lifted her right arm a couple of inches

from her side to indicate the gauze wrapped around the upper part of her limb. "I was grazed by one of the bullets."

Nicole sucked in a breath of air and her voice quavered slightly when she asked, "Are you okay?"

The corners of Merritt's mouth turned up. "I am. It's really just a superficial wound, although that's not how it felt when it happened. There was a lot of blood and I sort of panicked, but someone came over and helped me." Merritt cleared her throat and it was obvious to Claire and Nicole that talking about the incident was as difficult for Merritt as it was for them.

"Anyway," Merritt continued. "I want to thank you." She looked at Claire. "I was coming up the sidewalk on your left and I noticed that you seemed nervous and that you were glancing around."

Claire didn't realize that she'd been giving off such signals.

"I don't know why I noticed." A serious expression tugged at Merritt's face. "I'd worked late and I was walking home. I was really tired and I felt sort of out of it, distracted by what I'd been working on and still thinking it over in my head so I'm surprised that I noticed you at all, but somehow I picked up on your unease."

Claire and Nicole waited for Merritt to go on with her story.

"It all happened so fast. You lunged for your

friend." Merritt gestured to Nicole. "I was stunned for a second, but your actions combined with maybe me seeing the car tearing up the street caused me to follow your lead and I dropped to the ground." Picking up her cup, Merritt took a quick sip and then set it down. Claire could see the woman's fingers shaking. "One of the bullets grazed my arm as I fell." Merritt paused and swallowed. "It was a stroke of good fortune that you were on that sidewalk. I'm sure that I would have caught that bullet in the chest if you two weren't there last night." Merritt blinked fast a few times. "So, thank you. You saved my life."

CHAPTER 5

The three young women continued their conversation while Robby, pretending to sweep or clean, came by their table every chance he got to eavesdrop until Nicole gave him the evil eye and he scurried away. The rain and thunder carried on for another twenty minutes giving the girls the chance to talk without many customers in the shop.

"Did a detective come by to talk to you today?" Nicole lifted the glass of iced tea that Robby had dropped off on one of the snooping passes he'd made past their table.

Merritt nodded. "Yes. A Boston detective came to my office this morning to go over some details of the report I gave to the officers last night."

"Was it Detective Fuller?" Nicole asked.

"No, it was a Detective Mason. Valerie Mason. She asked me some unsettling questions." Merritt sighed. "I've been thinking about some of the questions for most of the day."

"Did one of the questions have to do with

whether someone you know might want you dead?" Claire shifted in her seat.

Merritt looked from Claire to Nicole. "Yes. Obviously the same question was posed to you."

"How did you answer?" Claire leaned forward to hear the reply.

Merritt bit her lower lip. "It's possible, I guess. I work for a law firm down on Castle Street in the Jasper Building and I'm at the State House a lot. The work I do is considered controversial by some ... victim advocacy, representing individuals in cases against big corporations. It can anger some people."

"I bet it can." Nicole made a face. "There must be big money involved in some of those court decisions. You rub some bigwigs the wrong way and, well ... who knows what someone might do?"

Merritt's jaw muscles tensed. "Before I joined this law firm, I worked for the state prosecutor's office. We tried some tough cases. We made some defendants plenty angry at us."

"Someone might be out for revenge?" Claire imagined that Merritt must have made more than a few enemies as a prosecutor and one of those enemies may have it in for her.

"It's certainly possible." Merritt fiddled with the handle of her coffee mug and then looked up with worried eyes. "What about either of you? Are any enemies lurking in your past?"

Nicole's forehead was lined with concern. "My boyfriend and I broke off our relationship of five years, but that happened over a year ago."

Claire turned to her friend. "But, he was the one who broke it off, not you."

"He did initiate the break up." Nicole seemed to be deciding whether or not to bring something up.

"But, what?" Claire asked. "Is there more to the story?"

"Brian got weird. He was so angry that I was working hard, trying to make a go of the café. Previously, he'd been supportive, but just before the shop opened, his personality took a turn. At first, I chalked it up to him feeling a little jealous over all the time I was devoting to the store, but he started acting oddly. He wouldn't go into work for days on end, he was reading all kinds of conspiracy things on the internet. He started to scare me."

Claire put a hand on her friend's arm.

"I asked Brian to go see his doctor. Needless to say, that did not go over well. I made an appointment for him and tried to take him to the doctor's office ... he had a fit and wouldn't go." Nicole brushed her hand over her eyes. "I was worried, I didn't know what else to do, so I called Brian's parents and they drove up. By this time, he'd broken off with me and I'd moved out of our apartment, but I felt I had to try and help. He went nuts when his parents arrived. His mom and dad had to call the police and an ambulance and he was taken to the hospital for observation."

"Good grief." Merritt shook her head.

"His mom called me. She said Brian couldn't be held without his consent. Brian left the hospital and they didn't know where he was. She told me to be careful."

"Have you seen him?" Claire's voice was full of concern.

"I haven't seen him for two months." Nicole lifted her hands in a helpless gesture. "But ... who knows?"

"He doesn't know where you live now, does he?" Claire was afraid that Nicole would go home some night and Brian would be waiting for her outside her apartment.

"He doesn't."

Merritt let out a long breath and turned her attention to Claire. "What about you? Is anyone lurking in the shadows waiting for you to pass by?"

Claire told her companions about Teddy's business associates and their attempts to contest his will, being very careful to downplay the amount of money and holdings that were actually involved. "I doubt that anyone is so angry that they'd be looking to shoot me." Claire hoped so, anyway.

Merritt pushed her dark hair over her shoulder. "Well, it seems that any of us could have been the target of the shooting."

An idea popped into Claire's head. "Or none of us was the target. It could have been random. Some guys were drunk or high and they decided to go scare some people. Maybe they didn't intend to shoot anyone at all. Maybe they shot high in the air, over everyone's heads, just to panic everybody. Maybe they got a kick out of it."

Nicole and Merritt stared at Claire, pondering her suggestion.

"It's possible." Merritt nodded.

"I guess it is." Nicole glanced across the shop and out the window. The storm had passed and the sun was shining causing steam to rise from the sidewalks as the rain water evaporated into the air. "It's odd to say this, but a random drive-by shooting would be better than one of us having some angry nut after us."

"Right." Merritt almost sighed with relief. "We wouldn't have to be looking over our shoulders waiting for something bad to happen."

A hopeful smile spread over Nicole's face. "Maybe the police will figure it out and arrest whoever was in that car. There were a lot of people on the sidewalk. Someone might have given the police a good description of the vehicle, someone might have seen the license plate. Maybe it will be solved in a few days and then we can forget about the whole thing."

Claire smiled at Nicole even though deep down

she didn't think anything would be solved so quickly, and really, she couldn't shake the nagging feeling that last night's episode was only the beginning of the trouble.

"I'd better get back to work." Merritt suggested that they share contact information and each one pulled out phones and tapped at the screens to add the names and numbers. Leaning forward, Merritt gave Claire and Nicole a warm smile. "Thank you again for being there last night." She extended her hand to shake with Nicole and then with Claire. "We'll keep in touch." Merritt strode out of the chocolate shop.

Nicole sucked in a breath. "What do you think?"

Claire was staring at the table and didn't say anything.

"Claire?"

"Huh? What did you say? I was thinking things over."

Nicole narrowed her eyes and scrutinized her friend's face. "What's wrong with you, besides the obvious? You look like you've seen a ghost."

Claire opened her mouth and then snapped it shut. A moment later, she said, "Nothing's wrong. I'm just thinking about things." That part was true, but there was something else that had spooked Claire. When Merritt had shaken her hand, Claire's skin felt prickly, like it was buzzing with energy and she almost wanted to pull away from touching

Merritt.

"Claire?" Nicole's tone demanded a real answer. "Don't be evasive. I can tell there's something more to what you're saying."

Claire blew out a breath and slumped against her chair back. "I need to tell you something." Keeping her voice to a near whisper, Claire revealed how odd she'd felt the previous night, on edge, her head buzzing, sensations of anxiety pulsing through her body. "I thought maybe I was getting a migraine or coming down with the flu or something. I felt terrible, nervous, uneasy, like I wasn't even connected to my body." She stared at Nicole waiting for her to scoff at the strange things she'd just reported.

"That's cool."

Claire blinked, stunned that Nicole accepted what she'd just heard, but also because her friend seemed to think it was interesting.

Nicole's eyes brightened. "You must have sensed that danger was coming. Wow. That's why you tackled me on the sidewalk. You had a premonition."

The color started to drain from Claire's face. "Oh, I don't think it was a premonition. No." She forced a chuckle. "It wasn't anything like that."

"Of course it was." Nicole's eyes were wide and she leaned close to Claire, her voice bubbling with excitement. "You have some sort of skill. Have you ever sensed something like that before?"

Claire sat up straight and nearly shouted. "No."

"Come on. Think back. I bet you've sensed things before, but maybe they weren't strong feelings and you dismissed them as déjà vu or a coincidence or something like that."

Claire's hands started to shake and a cold sweat formed on her back. She had had feelings like that. Plenty of times. And she had brushed them aside. People often told her that she had strong intuition. Suddenly, Claire's heart started to race remembering that the woman with the tarot cards had told her to pay close attention to her intuition and not to ignore it. How did she know?

"Have you?" Nicole asked. "Have you ever had strong feelings before?"

"I guess I have." Claire's voice was so quiet that it was almost impossible to hear what she'd said.

"This is super interesting." Nicole placed her hand on her friend's arm. "Maybe this skill of yours is going to keep us safe. Heck, it already has."

"It scares me. I don't know what's going on." Claire fiddled with her paper napkin ripping it into small pieces.

"You know, we should go see that woman who was in here with the tarot cards. She might be able to help you understand this thing of yours, how should we describe it, your skill ... ability?" Nicole smiled. "Maybe that woman can at least tell us what word to call it."

"Okay, maybe that's a good idea." Claire swiveled in her seat to face Nicole. "Because, when I shook hands with Merritt ... I...."

Nicole's brow furrowed as she looked at Claire's pale, worried face. "What happened when you shook her hand?"

Claire shifted her gaze and looked down at the table top. "When I shook hands with Merritt just now... I felt something. I felt something bad, something terrible, but I don't know what it means."

CHAPTER 6

"Robby, come over here." Nicole called across the shop.

Robby had a suspicious look on his face when he approached the table where Claire and Nicole were sitting.

"Sit down with us." Nicole gestured to the seat across from Claire.

"Why?" Robby gave his boss the eye.

"Help us with something."

"I don't know what you have planned, but whatever it is, I don't think it's a good idea." Claire's voice was firm.

Robby looked at Claire and thought that what they wanted from him might prove to be interesting if Claire didn't think it was a good idea, so he sat. "What do you need help with?"

"Nothing." Claire was about to get up when Nicole reached out and took her arm.

"Hold on. Let's do an experiment." Nicole turned her attention to the young man. "Claire has strong intuition. I think she could hone this skill into something useful."

Robby flicked his eyes to Claire and then back to Nicole. "Yeah?" he said slowly, not understanding.

"Let Claire hold your hand. Shake with her." Nicole flapped both of her hands at the two people indicating that they should clasp their right hands together.

"I don't think this is a good idea." Claire kept her hand in her lap.

"You said that already." Nicole slid her fingers under Claire's wrist and pushed up. "Go ahead. It can't hurt anything. Robby, shake with her. Make it a long handshake. Claire needs to practice."

Robby extended his hand over the table. "What's she supposed to do? Is she going to tell my fortune, or something?"

"Don't talk. Let's see what happens."

With a scowl on her face, Claire slowly lifted her arm and grasped Robby's outstretched hand.

"Close your eyes." Nicole encouraged her friend. "So you aren't distracted by anything."

Claire lowered her eyelids as Robby made eye contact with his boss. Putting her index finger to her lips, Nicole urged Robby to remain silent and the three sat quietly for nearly two full minutes with Nicole glancing to the shop door every few seconds hoping that no customers would come in and disturb the experiment.

Claire opened her eyes and released Robby.

"What happened?" Nicole was eager to hear what had transpired.

"We shook." Claire's face was neutral.

"Did you sense anything? Did you feel anything?"

"Yes. I felt Robby's hand in mine." Claire smiled and stood up. "I have to get home to Bear and Lady."

Nicole stood. "That's it? You felt nothing? Maybe you didn't hold on long enough. Maybe you should try again."

Robby checked the wall clock. "I need to go, too. I need to get to class." Robby attended a performing arts college studying vocal performance, guitar and piano, as well as the business-side of being an artist. Winking at Claire, he told her, "Maybe tomorrow we can hold hands again."

Claire removed her apron and chuckled. "Don't hold your breath."

With her hands on her hips and a disappointed frown on her face, Nicole stood listening to her employees banter until the two left the chocolate shop for the day and went in different directions down the sidewalk.

Heading in the direction of Beacon Hill, Claire called over her shoulder to Robby, "Good luck with your audition tonight."

Robby spun around and gaped at Claire as he watched her walk away.

He hadn't told a single soul that he had a tryout scheduled for later that night.

***

Claire brought the dogs to the Boston Common and as they wiggled and squirmed to be released, she struggled to flick the metal clasps to free them from their leashes. At last, the clasps clicked and the Corgis flew around the grassy hill chasing and being chased by four other dogs that had come with their owners for playtime. Sinking onto the grass, a huge smile spread over Claire's face as she watched the animals dodge and leap and take off like rockets. Claire stretched out her long legs and the warmth of the sun on her skin made her eyelids heavy tempting her to consider resting back for a quick a snooze.

Bear darted over to his owner and positioned himself a few feet away from her leaning down so that his front legs were flat on the ground and his butt was up in the air. Making eye contact with Claire, he let out a woof and then zoomed back to where the other dogs were playing leaving his owner chuckling at the speed the dog was capable of achieving despite his small legs.

Claire's mind wandered to the strange events of

the past two days and she shuddered when she thought about the gunshots that had been fired from the speeding car so close to her and Nicole. Images flashed in her head of the car, of the tarot card woman who had come to the chocolate shop, of Merritt Handley, and of Robby sitting across the table from her with a look of slight distrust as she took his hand. Her thoughts jumped around in her head so fast they were like a monkey leaping from one tree branch to another.

Despite telling her colleagues that she hadn't felt something when holding Robby's hand, she *had* picked up on little things that bounced into her mind in a way that almost made her think that Robby had verbally shared the information with her. Claire sensed Robby struggling with a difficult piano piece and felt his triumph when he finally mastered it and she picked up on his nervousness and apprehension over an important audition he was facing later in the day.

Slipping on her sunglasses, Claire puzzled over why she was suddenly experiencing these unusual sensations and premonitions. She'd always had intuition about things, she easily picked up on how people were feeling, and could sense if a situation seemed off. Claire knew right away when she'd met Teddy that they would be important to one another, but she'd never had perceptions that foretold of coming danger or sensations that were as powerful as the ones she'd had recently.

Claire stood up and stretched and started to jog around the periphery of the Common to try and clear her head. The two Corgis saw their owner head off and dashed to her side to run along with her for a minute before taking off again to play with the other dogs. The routine was always the same whenever Claire, Bear, and Lady went to the common ... the dogs raced with their canine friends, checked on their owner as she sat or jogged around, and bounced back to the hill to jump and play. Claire loved the dogs' exuberance and high-spirits and they always lifted her from fatigue or sadness and brightened her day.

Watching her two sweet animals charge around the grass, Claire had her head turned and only noticed at the last moment that she was about to plow into a pedestrian. She lurched to the side to avoid hitting the person.

"Claire?" The man who had been about to be mowed down had side-stepped to miss the head-on crash.

Claire stopped and turned to see Detective Ian Fuller standing in front of her. "Oh. Sorry."

"Is it your habit to run down pedestrians on city sidewalks?" Detective Fuller spoke with a serious tone, but then his face broke into a wide grin.

Claire began to blubber an apology until she saw that the man was kidding. "I'm training for a mini-triathlon. I have a lot of work to do."

Bear and Lady darted from behind a group of trees and bounced joyfully around the detective who bent down with a chuckle and scratched the dogs behind their ears. "Are they yours?"

Claire nodded. "They won't jump on you. They just like to dance around."

"That's lucky. I thought they might be like their owner and would attempt to knock me down and trample me."

As Claire let out a heart-felt laugh, she couldn't help but notice the detective's arm muscles rippling under his starched white shirt as he petted the dogs and she looked away embarrassed when she realized how blatantly she was gaping at the man. Wanting to steer her attention to something other than the detective's physique, she brought up the case. "Any news about that car and the gunshots from last night?"

Detective Fuller straightened. "It's still being investigated."

Claire knew that he wouldn't be able to share any details about the case, but she'd hoped that he might tell her that someone had been brought in and was in custody and that the whole thing could now be put to rest. She pulled her ponytail holder from her hair and her blond curls cascaded around her shoulders. "I have to admit that it was pretty unnerving when you asked me if there was anyone who wanted me dead."

The detective nodded and tried to be reassuring. "It's just a standard question when something like this happens."

"Nicole felt the same way when you talked to her. The event and the questioning, well it shook our sense of stability and security. I've never felt like a victim before." Claire sighed as she and the detective walked along the sidewalk together. "Do you think the people in that car will be caught?"

Detective Fuller turned his head and made eye contact with Claire. "I hope so." The phone in his pocket buzzed and when he removed it and read the message on the screen, his face hardened. He pushed at the phone and held it to his ear as he backed away from Claire raising a hand to gesture "goodbye." Speaking into the phone, Detective Fuller spun away and ran down the sidewalk.

Claire could hear sirens blaring from the direction that the detective was running towards, but she dismissed the emergency sirens as the reason for his abrupt departure. She was living in a city with sirens going off on a regular basis, but still, a funny feeling gripped her stomach.

Looking across the lawn, Claire spotted her Corgis still zooming about with the other dogs and she smiled to herself wondering where all that energy came from. Reaching to unsnap the two leashes she'd put around her waist like belts, Claire headed towards Bear and Lady to take them home when she halted in her tracks and put her hand to her chest. Her heart felt like it had dropped into her stomach and cold sweat ran down her back as she spun around to look in the direction that Detective Fuller had hurried off to. Gazing at the buildings that surrounded the Common, a horrible feeling of alarm seemed to punch her in the gut.

Two people standing a few yards from her were hunched together looking at a phone. "Look at this." The young woman tilted the phone so her companion could see the screen. "That's just a few blocks from here. Want to go down there and see what's going on?"

The two people started to walk away when Claire called to them, her heart pounding wildly. "Has something happened?"

The young woman held up her phone. "There's been a shooting. It's all over social media. Someone's been shot down on Castle Street."

Claire's throat constricted and she felt like she couldn't breathe. "Does it say where on Castle Street?"

The young woman spoke as she and her friend hurried off in the direction of the shooting. "In front of the Jasper Building."

Claire sank down onto the grass. The Jasper Building. *That's where Merritt Handley said she worked.*

CHAPTER 7

With the humidity growing heavier, Claire and her Corgis hurried through the streets of Boston and returned to the chocolate shop just as Nicole was exiting the building. Bending to greet the two friendly dogs, Nicole noticed Claire's face and stood straight. "What's wrong now?"

"There was a shooting in front of the Jasper Building. Just a few minutes ago. That's where Merritt said she works."

The blood drained out of Nicole's face and her voice shook. "Oh, no. Let's go down there."

"Do you think it's a coincidence? Maybe it has nothing to do with what happened last night." Claire handed Lady's leash to her friend.

"I don't know what would be worse, having this shooting tied to last night or to have this be independent of what happened last night. If it doesn't have anything to do with the shooting in front of the Old South Meeting House, then what's going on in the city?"

"Gangs?" Claire asked.

Nicole shook her head. "There isn't much of that in Boston. God, did the shooter from last night target Merritt as she was going back to work? Was Merritt the one he was after?"

They turned the corner onto Castle Street to see the crowd that had formed on the sidewalk across from the Jasper Building and the emergency vehicles clustered in front. Police had blocked the street from both ends and two officers stood in the road at the corner waving traffic away from turning down Castle. Two ambulances had parked askew at the sidewalk and Claire and Nicole heard the squawk and crackle of police walkie-talkies and radios as some personnel stood around the sidewalk taking photographs and measurements and others stood together in serious conversations or hurried back and forth from police cars to the building.

The young women led the dogs to the opposite sidewalk where they joined the other people watching the scene unfold.

"A woman was shot." A short, muscular young man dressed in a tank top and jeans that fell below his hips told Claire and Nicole. "They took her away."

Nicole asked. "Was she alive?"

The guy shrugged. "Don't know. There was a lot of blood."

"Were you here when it happened?" Claire took a step closer. "Did you see it happen?"

"Nah. I got here just after. The cops herded witnesses into the building."

Nicole pointed across the street. "There's Detective Fuller."

The detective stood next to a short, bald man in a suit listening intently to what the man was telling him. When Fuller looked up, he noticed Claire and Nicole at the edge of the crowd and nodded as he lifted his hand with his index finger extended to ask them to wait. After more discussion with the bald man and several officers, Fuller hurried across the street and gestured for Claire and Nicole to move with him to the corner away from listening spectators.

"Was it Merritt Handley who was shot?" Claire hated to ask the question and braced for the answer.

Hearing that Claire knew Merritt, a look of surprise passed over Fuller's face. "No, Ms. Handley's inside. You're acquainted with each other?"

"Merritt came to see us a few hours ago." Nicole's gaze was trained on the activity across the street. "She told the two of us that she was standing nearby on the sidewalk last night when the drive-by shooting took place."

"Merritt found out who we were. She wanted to

talk to us about the shooting." Claire knelt beside the dogs to reassure them when another police car pulled up to the building with its lights flashing and its siren blaring. Looking up at Fuller, she asked, "Do you think this is unrelated to last night?"

The detective said, "Ms. Handley was on the sidewalk about to enter the building when the shooter walked up and fired."

Claire's heart dropped. Merritt must have been the target. "He must have been close to her? Did she see him and run inside just in time?"

"She did see him. She saw the gun and she ran into the building. A woman had just stepped out of the lobby onto the sidewalk and she ended up catching the bullet that may have been intended for Ms. Handley."

"How is that woman? Will she survive?" Claire looked over to the building.

Fuller's face was drawn. "I don't know the extent of her injuries."

Claire thought of something and turned to the detective. "Did Merritt get a good look at the shooter?" Claire's tone was excited thinking that this could be a break in the case. "Did she recognize him?"

Fuller shook his head. "Ms. Handley noticed the gun and that's what she focused on. She said she didn't know the man. She told us that she wouldn't be able to describe him except in vague terms. Her eyes were focused on the gun."

"I would probably be so frightened by the gun that I wouldn't take any time to notice what the guy looked like. I'd just take off, try to escape as fast as I could." Nicole absentmindedly patted Lady's head. "*Was* it a guy?"

Detective Fuller nodded. "It was a male about five feet eight inches tall, according to Ms. Handley. She thought he was a young man, maybe in his late twenties or early thirties, but she said she couldn't be sure."

"Are there witnesses?" Claire hoped that someone walking or driving by might be able to provide a description of the shooter.

"Some. We'll see if any of them prove helpful." Detective Fuller waved to a man standing across the street and started to cross over to meet him. Claire could see the tension in the detective's facial muscles. "I'll be in touch with both of you soon." Fuller jogged to the other side.

Nicole gave Claire the eye. "Do you want to stay longer and hang around?"

"Maybe a little while longer."

The dogs sat quietly at the young women's feet watching the commotion taking place on the sidewalks.

Nicole tipped her head back and looked up to the higher floors of the Jasper Building. "So Merritt must be the target. That makes me feel better about my own personal safety, but saying such a thing makes me feel very guilty for being so selfish."

"I know." Claire looked around at the people in the crowd. "It's a relief to know the shooter wasn't aiming at either of us, but I feel awful for Merritt. Why would someone target her? Do you think it's because of some legal work she's done?"

"Who knows?" Nicole gave a little shrug of her shoulder. "There are nuts all around us. Someone could target us for the way we dress or because we made some guy's coffee wrong. Slights don't even have to be real. Someone might misperceive another person's actions or words or facial expression and think there's some intended slight involved. People manufacture reasons to hate others."

"That's so depressing."

Nicole reached over and grabbed hold of Claire's hand causing her friend to gape at her.

"What are you doing?" Claire extracted her hand from Nicole's grasp.

Nicole nearly whispered. "Am I safe?"

"What do you mean?"

"Come on, Claire. Last night, you had the impression that something might happen to me. Today when you shook hands with Merritt you felt something bad. Hold my hand and tell me what you feel." Nicole gently took Claire's hand. "Am I safe?"

Claire flicked her eyes around at the other people standing on the sidewalk and adjusted her stance to block their view.

"Concentrate," Nicole urged.

Claire breathed in a long breath of the warm, humid air. She became aware of her clammy skin and damp T-shirt and wished she was at home taking a nice cool shower. Holding Nicole's hand made Claire's palm start to sweat. After several minutes, the act of breathing slowly in and out created a sense of calm that flowed over her and the noise of the cars and people and the news crews became muffled and distant.

"Claire?"

Nicole's voice shook Claire from her tranquil state and she blinked at her friend.

"Did you feel anything?" Nicole studied Claire's face.

"I felt calm."

For a moment, Nicole looked confused and then an expression of relief washed over her. "Okay. That's good. You didn't feel anything bad? Nothing worried you?"

"Nothing." Claire shook her head, but then her eyes clouded and her shoulders slouched. "I should have warned Merritt."

"I know that sounds like it would have been a good idea, but what would you have said to her? By the way, I got this terrible feeling when we shook hands?" Nicole narrowed her eyes. "Merritt would have thought that you were crazy. She wouldn't have taken it seriously."

Claire glanced over to the opposite sidewalk. "I should have called Detective Fuller. I...."

"Right." Nicole shook her head. "That would have been even worse. He would have had you locked up." She touched Claire on the arm. "Let's get out of here."

The girls and the dogs walked away from the scene and headed in the direction of the Common.

Thoughts swirled in Claire's head. "If I get these feelings, what good are they if I don't use them to help people? How can I just stay quiet? Shouldn't I do something with them?"

Nicole didn't answer right away. "I guess you should. But what ... and how?"

CHAPTER 8

The young women returned to Claire's apartment in Adamsburg Square to make dinner and talk things over. The two Corgis sat at attention in the kitchen to watch the preparation of a chicken and vegetable stir fry and they wagged their little tails as Claire and Nicole bustled about chopping and cooking.

"I'm starving." Nicole scooped the chicken and veggies out of the pan and placed the ingredients over rice on a serving platter. The outside patio table was set with blue and white plates, napkins, and silverware. "It's good we made a dish that was quick to prepare."

Claire carried two glass mugs and two bottles of craft beer to the table and lit the jar candles. When the girls sat down at the table and began to gobble their meals, Bear and Lady hurried into the rear garden and sniffed around the fence that enclosed the small yard. Claire called to the dogs. "Come away from there." She glanced at Nicole. "There are two loose boards on the fence that I need to get fixed. Those two know they aren't supposed to push on the slats, but they're always sniffing around them."

The girls ate in silence for a few minutes until Claire said, "Who knew worrying about getting shot would increase our appetites." She sipped from her mug. "I was just thinking about sending a text to Merritt saying we both heard what happened today and hoped she was doing okay."

Nicole swallowed the last bite of rice from her plate. "Merritt said she wanted us to keep in touch with each other so I think it would be a thoughtful thing to do."

Claire went inside to retrieve her phone and sent off the message. Tapping at the screen, she said, "I'm going to see what the latest news is reporting about the incident at the Jasper Building."

The leaves in the Maple tree rustled in a soft breeze and shadows started to stretch across the yard as lights twinkled on in the windows of surrounding brownstones.

"It's such a lovely evening." Nicole sighed. "Too bad we can't just enjoy it."

Reading from the online news, Claire reported, "The woman who was shot today is in serious condition, but she is still alive. Her identity is being withheld pending notification of her family. This article reports the incident to be the second random shooting in the city in two days." Claire fiddled with one of her long curls. "They weren't random. Are they just saying that to throw off the shooter?"

"Most likely. They don't want to alert the guy that they have an idea who the target really is. Knowing who the target is might help figure out who the shooter is. I bet the police are deliberately withholding information."

"Hopefully, the authorities can figure out who might bear Merritt a grudge and then arrest the guy." Claire continued to read the news accounts. "The articles all say the same thing. Not one of them mentions Merritt by name." Placing her phone down on the table, Claire said, "Merritt had the idea that something she'd done in her job might have triggered the shooting. Someone might be trying to get back at her for some case she worked on."

"It would be really helpful if someone saw the shooter and could give a description."

Claire rested her chin in her hand. "What could make someone want to kill Merritt?" Looking across the small yard to the two dogs dozing in the grass, Claire felt a twinge of regret for the ease and safety of the life she'd had with Teddy, but quickly dismissed the feeling.

Growing up in North Carolina, Claire and her mother hardly ever felt any peace, with her mom working multiple jobs and Claire often alone until late in the evening. Money was either tight or nearly non-existent. The two were happy together though, sewing, cooking, baking, reading, making their tiny apartment pretty with some wildflowers they'd picked on the hill behind the town park and carefully placed in a tall drinking glass and set on the middle of their small wooden table. Claire's mom talked endlessly about the importance of education and Claire rose to the challenge and excelled in school, determined to free her mother from the crushing and never-ending fear of becoming homeless.

Bear lifted his head from his paws and Claire smiled. She was financially secure, she was healthy, she had a lovely apartment in a wonderful city, and she had a true friend, something she'd neglected in the past, never having time to get to know or go out with peers since she was always working, working, working to pull herself and her mother out of the pit of poverty.

Bear jumped to his feet and let out a low growl as he stared from his spot on the grass through the glass patio doors into the house. Lady woke from her nap and leapt up, standing close to Bear, following his gaze.

Nicole sat up straight as Claire pushed herself up from the table, a worried look on her face, her head turning from the dogs to the interior of the house. A moment later, her front door bell rang.

"Who could this be?" Nicole's voice shook as she

lifted the dinner knife from beside her plate and held it tightly against her palm.

Claire, starting for the door, noticed what Nicole had in her hand. "Nic, gee, hide it at least."

When Claire pushed the slider open, the dogs rushed inside from the garden and the two young women followed them to the front door.

"Who is it?" Claire pushed on the intercom button struggling to keep her voice even.

"It's me, Merritt." The tinny words crackled through the intercom's metal register.

As Claire turned the bolt, she shared a wide-eyed look with Nicole.

Merritt stood under the lights on the granite front landing wearing jeans and a light sweater, her dark hair held back in a long braid. "Can I come in?"

Claire shook her herself out of her surprise at seeing Merritt at her door. "Yes, please. Come in."

When Merritt walked into the hallway, Bear moved back a few steps and growled low in his throat.

"It's okay, Bear." Claire reached down and ran her hand over the dog's head, telling Merritt, "I just texted you a few minutes ago."

Merritt nodded. "I was out for a walk. When I got your text, I decided to make a detour and come here."

Nicole had her arms wrapped around herself and

the dinner knife was stuffed into the back pocket of her jeans. "How did you know where Claire lives?"

"I looked her up on the internet."

"It tells my address?" Claire's stomach muscles tightened.

"I searched the internet for your name. It listed this block of town homes. Your last name is on the mailbox." Merritt shrugged.

The group moved into the living room and the women took seats on the sofa and chairs. Bear and Lady sat near the door to the patio keeping watchful eyes on the visitor.

After some initial silence, Merritt said, "I guess now we know which one of us the shooter was after."

Sitting at the edge of her seat, anxiety shimmied through Claire's body. "Did you see the guy? Did you see his face?"

Merritt's chest heaved with a huge sigh. She looked at the floor. "I was hurrying back to work. When I left your shop, I had to go to the State House. I had a meeting to get to. When it was over, I hurried back to the office. I crossed the sidewalk to the front doors of the building. There was something ... something caught my eye and I turned just as I was about to push the door open. I saw a figure. I saw the hand holding the gun. Instinct took over and I lurched inside." Merritt's fingers shook as her hand passed over her forehead. She raised her eyes. "I thought it was me. I thought it was my involvement in a case that caused this. Someone is out to get me."

"Do you have any idea who might be behind it or what case it's related to?" Nicole asked.

"Not really." Merritt leaned back against the sofa cushion. "Who knows?"

"The police must be on it." Claire tried to sound encouraging. "The detectives will figure it out. They must have lots of experience investigating things like this."

Merritt raised an eyebrow and one side of her mouth turned down. "I'm sure they've investigated many situations like this, but did they ever solve any of them?"

The thought never occurred to Claire that law enforcement wouldn't be able to solve a case like this. People swarmed the streets of the city, day and night. How could someone shoot a gun at a woman in front of an office building without someone seeing him do it or someone seeing him flee? How could someone shoot from a car into a crowd without being noticed? Claire's chest tightened and when she spoke, her voice wasn't very forceful or convincing. "They must have solved other cases like this. They'll solve this one." Claire felt uneasy and uncomfortable.

"The police and the detectives will go over everything with you." Nicole leaned forward.

"They'll go over all the cases you've been involved with. They'll get to the bottom of it."

Claire offered Merritt something to drink, but she declined. "I'd better get home. When I read your text, I thought I'd come by and let you know I'm okay."

"Stay," Clair urged. "We can talk. Have a drink with us."

Merritt stood. "Thanks, but I'm worn out. I need to get home."

The three walked to the front door together and when Merritt was outside on the stoop, she turned around, the entryway light shining on her face. "Just in case, you two better stay on your toes. Keep your eyes open. You never know." Merritt hurried down the granite steps and along the sidewalk into the night.

Claire shut and locked the door.

"Why did she say that?" Nicole frowned.

Claire glanced at the two scowling Corgis sitting a few feet from her. "Do you trust her?" she asked Nicole.

Nicole's mouth hung open for a moment. "What? What do you mean? Why wouldn't I trust her? I don't know. Do you?"

Claire's blue eyes clouded. "I'm not sure. I don't think I do."

CHAPTER 9

The rest of the evening passed with the two young women discussing the situation. Claire couldn't fully explain to Nicole why she had reservations about trusting Merritt Handley and while she was answering Nicole's questions about her misgivings, something that had been picking at her took form in her brain. Shifting on the sofa to face Nicole, she leaned forward. "If you had been shot at today and you narrowly missed taking the bullet and you realized that you must be the target, would you go out in the dark and take a walk all by yourself just hours after the shooting?"

Nicole let Claire's words settle in her mind without responding because she didn't know what to say.

Claire told Nicole about her suspicions. "Wouldn't you be afraid to go out, alone, in the dark? Wouldn't you call a friend or a family member to stay with you for awhile? Is it wise to go strolling around the city when someone has just taken shots at you twice in less than forty-eight hours?"

"*I* wouldn't go out." Nicole was adamant about that. "Maybe Merritt doesn't have anyone in the area that she can call on. Or maybe her friends are away. Maybe she's angry and wants to prove to herself that the person isn't going to make her reclusive, that the person isn't going to take her freedom away."

"It seems dumb. She doesn't strike me as dumb."

"So what are you saying?" Nicole asked.

"I don't know what I'm saying. I'm just questioning why Merritt would go out. Maybe she has poor judgment." Claire took a strand of her hair and twisted it between her thumb and index finger. "Isn't it odd that Merritt was near my house when she got my text? It's a big city."

"You're scaring me." Nicole shifted her eyes to the dark windows and glanced over her shoulders. "She might live nearby and that's why she was in the neighborhood."

"Her showing up on my doorstep made me uneasy." Claire shook her head. "I suppose I'm just feeling suspicious. I'm letting my mind run away with me."

With confusion and worry muddling their ideas, the young women called it a night and Nicole left the townhouse to head home, but not before making requests to borrow a big flashlight and the dinner knife that was still in her back pocket. Claire offered her friend the guest room, but Nicole declined wanting nothing more than to fall asleep in her own bed. Nicole chuckled when Claire offered to walk her home. "Then I'll have to walk you home and then us walking each other back and forth between our apartments will go on all night."

A fitful night's sleep caused Claire to rise bleary-eyed and weary wishing she could go back in time and erase the past two days from ever happening. The new, sudden strength to her intuition was unnerving and unexplainable, and desperate to understand it, Claire planned to ask Nicole for the name and address of the woman with the Tarot cards who had visited the chocolate shop the other day so that she could talk to her about what was happening. The morning was hot and already the air felt moist, heavy, stifling, and oppressive and little beads of sweat had formed on Claire's skin. She pushed the door open to the Adamsburg Deli and Market, located two blocks from her townhouse at the bottom of the hill, and the two Corgis rushed inside to greet the owner.

Tony Martinelli, tall and burly with a full head of white hair and tanned skin that gave the impression that he'd worked outside his whole life even though he hadn't, had owned the corner store for over fifty years. It was a small market and deli that also had a cramped self-service beverage counter tucked into one corner in front of several tables and chairs. Tony bent to pat the dogs and retrieved two dog bones from a basket near the cash register. Bear and Lady sat at attention with their two tails wagging back and forth, their eyes glued to the treats in Tony's hands. Tony put the bones on the floor in front of the animals and when he winked, the two leaned down and gobbled them up. "Where've you been?" He looked across at Claire.

Claire took the dogs and made a trip down the hill to the deli every morning before she went to work at the chocolate shop to get a cup of coffee and one of Tony's homemade granola bars. There was something about the man's coffee that no one else could replicate. Claire smiled. "We only missed yesterday morning."

"I notice when my two favorite dogs don't come in." Tony bustled behind the counter.

Claire frowned. "What about when I don't come in?"

Tony teased. "Oh, you weren't here yesterday? I didn't notice."

Claire smiled and shook her head as she poured a cup of coffee from the carafe on the counter. "Where is everyone?" Every day, there was a steady stream of regulars who stopped in on the way to work or to shoot the breeze.

"You're early. You beat the others by a half

hour."

Claire carried her cup to the side of the counter where Tony was stocking some shelves. "I couldn't sleep so I got up."

"Worried about something?" Tony eyed the pretty blond.

Claire shrugged. She and Tony had gotten to know each other over the past year, each one feeling a strong connection to the other. They'd shared stories about the past, talked about family, work, things that were important to them. Besides her mother, Claire had never really opened up to anyone the way she did with Tony, not even with Teddy. Tony felt like a kindred soul, almost like family.

"You heard about those shootings?" Tony emptied a case of candy and broke down the cardboard container with his big hands. "You be careful, Blondie. Stay aware of your surroundings."

Claire sighed and told him about being at the first shooting and what she knew about the two events. While she gave him the details of the story, Tony stood in front of her with the cardboard in his hands just staring at Claire, his eyes wide. "What's gone wrong in the world? What's wrong with people?"

"There have always been people like this." Claire took a swallow from her cup.

"I wonder. Things seemed safer years ago. We

didn't even lock our doors in the neighborhood." Tony had grown up in Boston's North End with four brothers and his parents sharing a small apartment. Claire had heard stories of neighborhood parties, delicious Italian food, kids playing outside with other kids, being poor, tight-knit families and friends, silly teenage brawls, and neighbors helping and relying on each other. Claire could relate to the being poor part, but the rest of Tony's growing-up years sounded like Heaven to her.

The corners of Claire's lips turned down. "Well, we need to lock them now."

"Keep these dogs near you. Don't walk around alone. You call me if you need me." Tony's brown eyes were serious. "Get some pepper spray."

"I'm not the target."

"Get some anyway."

Claire smiled inwardly at how pepper spray wouldn't be much help when facing a gun, but Tony's kind, concerned words and his worried eyes warmed her heart and she told him that she already had some and carried it at night and whenever she went out exercising.

The door opened and in walked Augustus Gunther, a slim, bent but spry older man with light blue eyes and thin silver-gray hair. He was dressed in trousers, a suit jacket, and a necktie. Claire always marveled how the man could be so dressed up even on the hottest days and never seemed to break a sweat. Augustus, ninety-one years old, was a former state supreme court judge and lived in a beautiful townhouse on Beacon Hill. He nodded to Tony and Claire and gave the Corgis a smile and a pat on their heads. “Good morning.”

Claire and Tony returned the greeting and while the man settled into one of the chairs, Tony hurried to the beverage counter to pour a cup of coffee for the judge. Augustus Gunther was the only person that Tony waited on, everyone else helped themselves.

Claire sat with Augustus, and Bear and Lady came to lie down at his feet. Topics of conversation touched on world events, books, documentaries, politics, and whatever was happening in the city. Augustus had recently picked up the hobby of baking and he enjoyed picking Claire’s brain about recipes and why something he’d done did not turn out quite right.

“You’ve heard the news?” Augustus looked pointedly at Claire and held his coffee mug up to his lips.

Claire nodded. “About the two shootings?”

“I mean the latest trouble.”

Bear stood up and edged closer to the man’s chair so that Augustus would pat his head.

Tony came over to the table. “What latest trouble?”

Claire held her breath and waited to hear what had happened.

"A woman was found in the Public Garden." Augustus's light blue eyes looked from Claire to Tony.

"What do you mean, Gus?" Tony was the only one who called the judge "Gus".

"A passerby found a woman facedown in the Swan Boat pond."

"When?" Claire couldn't hide her shudder.

"This morning around 5am."

"Dead?" Tony scowled.

Augustus raised an eyebrow. "Yes."

A barrage of questions ensued and the judge answered them with what he knew from the news reports. "The authorities believe the woman to be in her sixties. Dead, cause of death is unknown at this time."

Tony made eye contact with Claire. "At least it doesn't have anything to do with the recent shootings."

Claire's stomach felt queasy. She wasn't so sure it didn't.

CHAPTER 10

Claire and Nicole stepped off the bus into Harvard Square in Cambridge and made their way around tourists and students to a house off of Brattle Street where the Tarot card woman lived. Walking past restaurants and shops, they began to enter a more residential area of the street which was lined with large Colonial homes fronted by green lawns and flower beds overflowing with blooms. On their right, the young women walked by the former home of Henry Wadsworth Longfellow an American poet who lived in the house for nearly fifty years. From the summer of 1775 until April of 1776, General George Washington used that home as his headquarters during part of the American Revolution. The massive yellow house was built in 1759 in the mid-Georgian style and had white trim and black shutters and was now an historic landmark open to the public for tours.

Claire and Nicole turned onto the street they were looking for and found the home they wanted standing two houses from the corner.

Claire looked up at the large Victorian and swallowed hard before walking up the steps to the front porch where she rang the bell with a shaking hand. “I feel like running away.”

Nicole put her hand on her friend’s shoulder. “It’ll be okay. It will be helpful.”

The front door opened and Tessa Wilcox, the Tarot card lady, stood before them with a welcoming smile. “Hello again. It’s nice to see you both.” Gesturing to the right of the foyer, she led the girls into a beautiful parlor where they settled onto a deep green, velvet carved-back sofa. The room was lined with cherrywood bookshelves and a side table with a large cut-glass vase full of flowers stood in front of a window with yellow drapes hanging on each side. A small rectangular coffee table sat on an antique carpet woven of muted rose and green colored fibers. There was a silver tray in the middle of the table with a carafe of ice water and three glass goblets next to a plate of sugar cookies.

Tessa sat in a comfortable high-backed chair across from the girls. “Please, help yourself.” Looking from Claire to Nicole, the woman asked, “What brings you to me today? A reading? Some questions?”

Claire and Nicole exchanged looks.

“I have a few things I’d like to ask.” Claire’s

voice sounded raspy and she cleared her throat and poured some water into a glass so that she could sip.

"I thought you might." Tessa nodded. Her eyes were friendly and warm. "What would you like to know?"

Letting out a sigh, Claire said, "I don't even know where to begin."

Nicole sat at the edge of the seat. "Claire has recently had some experiences where when she touches someone she gets a feeling from them. She sensed that we were in danger the other night and her actions saved the two of us from injury."

The young women took turns relaying the tales of the shooter passing by the Old South Meeting House and the man who approached Merritt Handley at the office building with a gun in his hand.

"I sense that you've always had strong intuition about things. Is that correct?" Tessa asked.

Claire nodded. "I never paid much attention to it until recently when my feelings have become stronger. Thinking back on the past, I can see now that there were certain times when I had a sensation or knew something that others didn't. But I don't understand why this is happening. I'm thirty-five years old. Why is this, whatever it is, suddenly becoming stronger?" Claire's eyes glistened with emotion and she blinked hard several times.

"Have you had a recent injury?" Tessa looked squarely at Claire who shook her head. "Have you lost consciousness recently, however briefly?"

Again Claire shook her head.

"Have you suffered an emotional upset?"

Claire froze. "My husband passed away a year and half ago."

"Ah. I'm very sorry for your loss." Tessa gave a slight nod. "Sometimes a person's abilities increase after an emotional upheaval. Other times, a person who has abilities *lose* those skills after an emotional or stressful event. Why this happens, no one really knows. After the loss of your husband, did you notice premonitions or sensations becoming stronger?"

Claire's eyes narrowed as she considered the question. Squeezing her hands together in her lap, she said, "I think you're right. I thought the heightened feelings were due to my grief. I dismissed many of my feelings as nonsense, attributing them to my being in such an emotional state."

"Tell me about the things you feel." Tessa relaxed against the sofa.

Claire explained how, at times, she felt that something bad was going to happen, and at other times, she had premonitions about good things coming. "Sometimes when I hold a person's hand, I can pick up a little bit about them, like I felt a colleague's nervousness and knew he had an important audition coming up." Claire made eye contact with Nicole. "I felt that Nicole might be harmed when we went out together the other night. Yesterday, I felt danger when I held the hand of the woman who was shot at outside the Jasper Building. Once on Nantucket, I sensed that an antique woven basket that was on display in a museum had been made right there on the island by a Wampanoag Native American hundreds of years ago. It hasn't been proven, but I believe that I'm right about it." Claire glanced out the window thinking about the past sensations.

Tessa spoke. "There are things that float on the air unseen."

Claire turned her eyes to the woman.

"The unseen things are almost like electric currents or areas of high and low pressure. We don't see those things, but they're there. Some people feel the currents of information and are able to extract details from them."

"Huh," Nicole said. "That's an interesting way to think about Claire's skills. It makes it less weird."

Claire gave her friend a scowl.

Tessa added, "The current stretches forward and backward, into the future and back into the past. Each person who has these skills, we might call them a seer or intuit, seems to have a certain distance available to him or her. For instance, I have a friend who is able to see decades into the past, but another person I know is only able to look back a few days into the past."

Claire asked, "Can I control it so I don't feel anything if I don't want to? If I touch someone, I might not want to know about bad things because, really, what would I say? Oh, by the way, tomorrow you'll be hit by a bus. How could I ever explain such a thing?"

Tessa smiled. "I understand. I can teach you some ways to block it. One way is to hold your breath and push down slightly into your chest. Sort of bear down. It will take practice, but you'll be able to keep sensations at bay whenever you don't want to look into the invisible current."

A look of relief washed over Claire's face. She wanted to be able to control this skill, not have it control her, and hearing that there were ways to prevent the thoughts and sensations from popping into her head comforted her.

Tessa told her guests about people she knew with many different kinds of skills and Claire and Nicole sat listening, enthralled, for over an hour. Tessa checked the time. "I have a client arriving in a few minutes. I'd be happy to have you both return again if there are other questions or concerns that come up later." She smiled kindly at Claire and winked. "Practice your control and later, there are other things that I can teach you that might prove helpful."

When they reached the front porch, Claire wrestled with a question that she'd wanted to ask. As Nicole walked down the steps, Claire turned around and whispered, "The woman who was found dead in the Public Garden this morning. Is she linked to the shootings?"

Tessa held Claire's eyes. "Some things you have to find out on your own."

***

"Did you ask her?" Nicole walked briskly along side Claire. "Did you ask her about the dead woman found this morning?"

Claire told Nicole how Tessa replied when asked about the dead person in the Public Garden and whether she might be connected to the shootings.

"She said you need to figure it out on your own?" Nicole frowned. "For Pete's sake. That isn't helpful. Wouldn't it be in everyone's best interests to tell if the incidents are linked?"

"Maybe she doesn't know."

"I didn't think of that." Nicole pushed her hair over her shoulder. "I thought this invisible current-thing that Tessa talked about seemed like a book that people like you could take a look at, but maybe some chapters are closed. Maybe you people can only read certain chapters."

"Please don't refer to me as *you people*." Claire shuddered. "It's like I'm in some sort of strange club."

Nicole raised an eyebrow and gave Claire a look. "Well...."

Claire let out a groan. After a few minutes of walking, Claire said, "Talking to Tessa made me feel better about this ... skill. Maybe I'll be able to control it so I can't feel anything if I don't want to. Maybe I can eventually use it to help people. I need to figure it all out."

"Did your mother have this intuition?" Nicole asked.

Stopping short, Claire stared at her friend and said slowly, "I don't know."

"Your mother might have had it, but might not have understood it. Maybe it frightened her, so she didn't say a word."

Although Claire missed her mom every day, this was one of the moments when she longed for her mother and wished that she was still alive. *Did she have intuition? Did I inherit it from her?*

The young women started walking again and Nicole asked, "What about your father?"

"I didn't know him." Claire's voice was brusque and she stared straight ahead.

"Grandparents?"

"They died before I was born."

"Any siblings, cousins, aunts, or uncles you could ask about it?"

"There isn't anyone. I'm alone."

Nicole bumped her elbow against Claire's arm and smiled at her. "No. You're not."

CHAPTER 11

The woman who had been shot outside the Jasper Building was identified in news reports the next morning as Siobhan Ellis, thirty-six, a paralegal who worked at the same firm as Merritt Handley. Despite having been shot in the upper right chest, Siobhan's condition had been upgraded and she was now allowed visitors. Claire had decided to make a detour to the hospital after work. She didn't know why she kept it to herself, but she didn't share her intentions with anyone else.

Picking up a floral arrangement in the hospital gift shop, Claire took the elevator to the fourth floor and found Siobhan's room at the end of the corridor.

The trim-looking woman had shoulder-length auburn hair and was sitting up in bed looking out the window. Her right arm was in a sling. She turned her head when she saw Claire coming into the room, noticed the flowers, and nodded to the empty bed next to hers assuming Claire had come to visit the person who had occupied the room with her. "Eliza was discharged this morning."

Claire looked confused for a second and then said, "Oh, I came to see you."

Now it was Siobhan's turn to look confused. "Have we met?"

Claire placed the flowers on the side table and gestured to the chair next to the bed. "May I?" Claire sat. "We haven't met. I hope you don't mind that I came by to see how you're feeling. My friend and I were in the line of fire the night before the shooter showed up at the Jasper Building yesterday. We were near the Old South Meeting House when a car drove by and shot at us as we stood on the sidewalk. I hope you're okay. I was worried when I heard what happened and since we were both caught up in similar situations, I just wanted you to know that I was thinking about you and wishing you well."

"That's very nice." Siobhan smiled. "I guess you're better at ducking than I am."

Claire returned the smile and introduced herself. She asked how the woman was doing and Siobhan gave her an account of her injuries and her prognosis. "The bullet missed everything important, thank heavens. It hurts like heck though." Narrowing her eyes, she said, "You heard about the dead woman they found in the Public Garden? You think it's connected to the person who shot at us?"

"It seems quite the coincidence, doesn't it?" Claire frowned. "Three shootings, three days in a row?"

"I'm suspicious." Siobhan leaned her head back against the pillow. "The detective said I probably wasn't the target, so at least I don't have to be looking over my shoulder once I get out of here."

"Did he tell you who he thinks the target is?"

"He didn't want to say, but since Merritt Handley was standing right near me, I'd venture a guess that she might be the one."

Claire nodded. "I'd bet the same thing since Merritt was near me and my friend the night of the shooting. You and Merritt work at the same firm. Do you have any idea why someone might be trying to kill her?"

Siobhan's face clouded. "There are probably lots of reasons."

That wasn't what Claire expected to hear. "Why? Because of the cases she's worked on?"

Siobhan sighed. "That, yes, and because she can be difficult. She isn't a team player. She only looks out for herself. She's cutthroat. She'd run over her own mother to get to the top. It wouldn't surprise me at all if people were waiting in line to take Merritt Handley down."

"Does she get along with *anyone* in the firm?"

Cocking her head and raising an eyebrow, Siobhan said, "The partners."

"How do *you* feel about her?" Claire wondered if Merritt was only in competition with the other lawyers and treated the office staff differently.

"She isn't pleasant with anyone. She doesn't make small talk. She's demanding and rude to the paralegals and the office staff. People would prefer to avoid her." Siobhan shifted against the pillows. "A person can progress in a career without being awful to colleagues. One of the lawyers, her daughter got sick at school and she asked Merritt to cover for her for an hour. Merritt told one of the partners that the woman left without asking anyone to cover. She went on to say that she had reservations about the woman's dedication to the firm. She planted seeds of doubt about the woman in the partner's mind. That's what she is like. Subtle things, but consistent little things add up. There isn't any reason to do that. None at all."

"But are those things enough to make someone want to kill her?" Claire couldn't believe that someone would risk all they had to commit murder against a conniving colleague.

Siobhan shrugged. "People can get pushed beyond reason."

"Is there someone you think might be responsible for the shootings?"

"I have no idea." Siobhan shook her head. "I really hope it isn't someone I work with. God."

"What about her cases?" Claire asked. "Could

someone be so angry about a law case that Merritt handled that they might want her dead?"

"It's law." Siobhan's face was serious. "Legal decisions can infuriate people."

"Did you get a look at the shooter?"

Siobhan's face lost its color and she looked across the room at nothing. Claire didn't think she was going to reply, but then she said in a voice just above a whisper, "Something about him seemed familiar. What it was, I don't know. The whole thing took a few milliseconds. I was running out for a quick errand to the pharmacy to pick up something for one of the partners. I hurried through the lobby and pushed through the glass doors." Siobhan hesitated. "It seemed like everything slowed, like things were in slow motion. I barely noticed Merritt. We didn't say anything to each other. She had a look on her face, like something was terribly wrong. I stepped past her just as I noticed her expression." Siobhan sucked in a deep breath and winced from the pain in her chest. "Out of the corner of my eye, I saw movement. The gunman had his hand up. He was holding the gun." A shudder ran through the woman on the bed. "I whirled. I heard the roar of the gun being fired. That's all I remember. I woke up here, in the hospital."

Claire leaned forward. "What seemed familiar about the gunman?"

Siobhan narrowed her eyes and turned her head to Claire. “I don’t know. A combination of his height, his build, the way he moved....” She shook her head. “He was wearing baggy jeans, a baggy shirt. He had a winter cap pulled over his hair. He wore gloves and sunglasses.”

Claire waited.

“Maybe I don’t know him at all.” Siobhan shook her head slowly, her auburn hair moving against the pillow. “I don’t know. It’s just a feeling I had.”

“I think it’s important to listen to intuition.” Claire held Siobhan’s eyes. “Maybe something about him will come to you. Maybe you’ll remember something that will identify him.”

“I think we should keep in touch.” Siobhan asked Claire to exchange contact information and then she rested her head back and closed her eyes for a moment. Claire was about to say goodbye so that the woman could rest, when a tall man entered the room. He was dressed in an impeccably tailored dark navy suit, white starched shirt, and blue and red tie. His posture was straight and he had an authoritative bearing. His sandy hair was cut close to his head and showed some gray at the temples. He and Claire glanced at each other as Siobhan opened her eyes and saw the visitor. “Oh. Mr. Freeman.”

“How is our favorite paralegal?” A broad smile formed over his face and Claire immediately thought it looked fake.

Siobhan pushed herself up a bit in the bed. "I'm doing well, thanks, Mr. Freeman."

The man made a show of the huge flowering plant he was carrying and Siobhan thanked him and gestured to the windowsill. "It's lovely."

When Freeman walked to the window to place the plant, Siobhan quickly turned her head to Claire and with wide eyes, mouthed the word, "Stay."

Introductions were made and Alex Freeman sat down in the chair on the other side of the bed looking uncomfortable. "I can only stay a few minutes. Meetings." Freeman was a partner at the law firm where Siobhan worked. "So sorry this happened to you, my dear. You'll be as good as new and back to the office before you know it." He winked. "I don't know how we'll manage until you're back." The man turned his attention to Claire. "This woman runs the entire firm, you know. The rest of us, well, we aren't important at all. Siobhan is the one we can't do without."

Claire nodded and didn't know what to say.

"How do you know Siobhan?" Freeman's tone was almost demanding.

Claire straightened in her seat to full height and looked Freeman in the eye. In her previous career as an attorney, she was used to assumptions and condescension and challenges and that's what she felt Freeman was giving off so she answered vaguely. "Siobhan and I have some things in common. Those things brought us together."

Freeman seemed about to ask what the things were that brought them together, but his question was interrupted by Siobhan. "How is Merritt? How is everyone in the office handling what happened?"

Freeman cleared his throat. "It was most unfortunate. People were shaken by it. They all send their hopes that you are on the mend and will soon be back at work." He nodded and smiled again. Leaning forward, he said, "It's just terrible. What did the gunman look like?"

The abruptness of the question took Siobhan by surprise. She opened her mouth to say something, but nothing came out.

"Did you get a look at him?" Freeman's forehead creased. "Can you describe him?"

Claire watched the interaction with concern. Siobhan's chin dipped and she didn't make eye contact with the man while the intensity of Freeman's stare seemed out of place and inappropriate. Claire wondered, if in his legal work, the man used his penetrating gaze to unsettle whoever he was questioning.

"No." Siobhan's voice was meek. "I can't describe him. It happened too fast. I didn't get a good look at him."

Claire raised an eyebrow surprised at the woman's response. Clearly, Siobhan did not want to share any information about the gunman with her boss.

Freeman continued his interrogation. "Really? Nothing? How was he dressed?"

"I don't recall. It happened so fast." Siobhan folded her hands together and placed them on her stomach before closing her eyes.

A nurse came into the room to check Siobhan's vitals and Claire stood up and looked at Freeman. "I think Siobhan needs to rest."

The nurse agreed. "Visits should be short until she gets some of her strength back."

Freeman said, "I need to get back to the office." Saying a few encouraging words to his employee, the law partner gestured for Claire to exit the room ahead of him.

Claire nodded and wished Siobhan well. She would have to return another time to ask Siobhan the reason why she didn't reveal any details of the gunman to Freeman. An idea popped into Claire's head as the nurse closed the door to Siobhan's room. Claire stopped and turned, extending her hand to Freeman. "It was nice to meet you."

Freeman took her hand and pumped. "Likewise." He nodded and strode away down the hall.

Claire watched him go. She didn't like what she felt when she held his hand.

CHAPTER 12

Claire stood in the back room of the chocolate shop absentmindedly folding the sour cream into the mixture thinking about her visit to the hospital yesterday to visit with Siobhan Ellis.

"You look a million miles away." Nicole bustled to the refrigerator to get a gallon of milk.

"I'm thinking." Claire looked to the front room of the shop to be sure Robby was busy and waved Nicole over to the counter. She told her friend about Siobhan and the partner from the law firm, Alex Freeman.

"Why didn't you tell me you were going? I would have come along." Nicole leaned against the counter.

"You had an appointment yesterday afternoon. I wanted to go meet the woman and get a sense of things." Claire lowered her voice. "Siobhan thinks the gunman seems familiar, but she doesn't know how or from where she might know him. It might pop into her head one day. What she said about

Merritt though complicated things. I thought the trouble might revolve around a case that Merritt had worked on and that could still be the reason that someone is after her, but her behavior in the office and the way she treats the people she works with could be another reason she is being targeted." Claire's face clouded. "That lawyer, though, Alex Freeman, something seemed off with him."

"How so?" Nicole asked.

"He seemed phony, saying how Siobhan ran the whole office, his flattery seemed over the top."

"He might just be awkward in situations like that," Nicole offered.

"But...." Claire began.

Robby walked in to pick up some clean plates for the front room shelves. He glanced at Claire and Nicole and realized that their conversation had halted when he entered the room. Eyeing them, he said, "Discussing my handsome good looks?"

"Yes," Claire told the young man with an even tone of voice.

"Keep it up then." Robby left the room.

"So this Freeman guy left Siobhan's room with me," Claire picked up her story. "I decided to shake his hand to see if I could pick up on anything."

"Ohh," Nicole said eagerly and took a step closer to Claire. "Did you ...?"

Claire nodded. "I felt something. When I shook with him, I had an overwhelming sense of distrust, bad intentions, like he was up to something, like he was involved in something bad. I wanted to pull my hand away and wash it off."

Nicole considered what Claire had just reported. "He might not have anything to do with Merritt and the gunman though. He might be crooked or dishonest or involved in some corruption."

"I know, but I got the distinct feeling that it had something to do with Siobhan or Merritt."

"What a tangled web." Nicole shook her head.

Robby stuck his head into the room. "I hate to disturb your important conversation, but am I the only one working here today? We've got a crowd out front."

Nicole and Claire hurried to the front of the store to wait on customers and, for the next few hours, there was hardly a break in the flurry of people to be served. Claire's new strawberry cheesecake was a huge hit and sold out before lunchtime. When things slowed, the shop crew cleaned and refilled the bakery cases.

"Whew. I'm going to need to hire more help if things keep going like this. It's never been busier." Nicole carried a serving tray of mini eclairs to the refrigerated case.

Claire smiled. "It's a good problem to have."

"I've been thinking of having you concentrate on the baking and preparation and hiring someone to just take orders and serve. You have a real talent."

Nicole wiped down the counter.

"Whatever works best is fine with me." Claire noticed two older men sitting by the window and one of them raised his finger and caught her eye. Walking to their table, Claire heard a snippet of their conversation.

"Did you hear the news reports?" The older man who wore glasses asked his companion. "The woman from the Public Garden has been identified. Sixty-two years old. She had some relation to a person who was outside the Jasper Building when that gunman showed up."

Claire interrupted. "Do you know the woman's name? The woman from the Public Garden?"

Dark brown eyes looked at Claire through thick glass lenses. "I didn't catch it."

"The dead woman had some connection to a person who was outside the Jasper Building when the gunman showed up there?" Claire wanted to be sure she'd heard correctly.

"Yes." The gray-haired man nodded. "Don't you find that odd? Do you think the gunman at the Jasper Building killed the woman who was found in the park?"

Claire looked out the shop's big window, thinking. "I wonder."

"I bet these things are tied together," the man opposite the eyeglass wearing man said. "I'd bet the same person is responsible for all this recent trouble." The man gave a shudder.

Claire wasn't sure if the same person was involved in the shootings and the murder of the woman in the park, but she felt positive that there was a link between the three events. She just didn't know what that link could be.

***

Claire brought Bear and Lady to the Common and while they played and dashed about with the other dogs, she ran around the perimeter of the grassy area several times to log four miles, all the while keeping an eye on the two Corgis. After their outing, the three went home so Claire could shower and then they walked down the hill to Tony's Deli.

"Yeah, I heard the news," Tony said while stacking a section of the shelves with cans of tomato paste. "The woman was sixty-something, a hairstylist. She owned a small salon off of Newbury Street. She had a customer the other night and was running late. She called her husband to tell him she was finishing up at the salon and would be leaving in ten minutes. She never arrived home."

The Corgis sat on each side of Tony supervising the man's work.

Claire, perched on a step stool, sipped from her cup of tea. "Supposedly, the hairstylist has some connection to someone who was at the Jasper

Building at the time of the shooting."

"I heard that." Tony broke down the cardboard box that had contained the tomato paste cans. "The news report didn't say the name of the person though. I bet the cops are keeping that under their hats."

"What was the hairstylist's name?" Claire asked.

Tony shrugged. "I don't recall. I do know they said the name of the salon was *Amore*."

"Amore?" Claire sat up straight. "I used to go there when I went to law school in Cambridge ten years ago. Was the woman's name Alicia?"

Tony rubbed his chin. "Maybe?"

Claire stood up and took her phone from the counter. "The owner of that salon used to be Alicia Fitchburg." With shaking fingers, Claire tapped at the phone screen trying to find a news article reporting the name of the woman who had been found in the Public Garden. A minute passed and then Claire gasped as her arm dropped to her side, her wide eyes focusing on Tony. With a shaky voice she said, "It's right here. She's the one. Alicia Fitchburg. She's the dead woman."

"You knew her?" Tony gaped.

"She did my hair for three years while I was going to law school." Claire sank back onto the step stool. "Why Alicia? Why would someone kill her? What connection could she have to someone who was at the Jasper Building?"

Tony folded his strong arms across his chest. "What was she like? Did you ever get the notion she was into anything she shouldn't have been?"

"What do you mean?" Claire's forehead creased.

"Drugs? Did she sell out of the salon?"

"I never saw anything like that." Claire was adamant. "She wouldn't do anything like that."

Tony dipped his chin and leveled his eyes at Claire. "Just because you didn't see it, doesn't mean it wasn't going on. Think back. Did you ever hear or see anything that caught your attention, that seemed out of place?"

Claire's mouth turned down. She couldn't believe that Alicia Fitchburg would have been involved in illegal activities. "It was years ago. Nothing like that stood out. Never."

"Well, something got her killed." Tony retrieved another box of goods from the store room.

"Maybe she ran into a nut." Claire scratched Bear's ears.

Tony raised an eyebrow. "Seems it was the same nut who shot at you and Nicole."

"Maybe." Claire's thoughts twirled round and round like they were tethered to a carousel. "I need to find out how Alicia was connected to the shooting at the Jasper Building."

"Don't you go pushing your nose into this." Tony's voice was stern. "You got no business sniffing around. I mean it, Blondie. Keep out of it."

Claire's voice was soft. "I think I'm already in it."

CHAPTER 13

Claire wore a short-sleeved black dress and had her curly locks pulled up into a soft bun as she walked up the steps to the funeral home with her palms sweaty and her heart pounding. Although she hadn't seen Alicia Fitchburg for more than ten years, she felt an affinity for the woman who had cut and straightened her hair while she was in law school and she wanted to pay her respects.

Claire enjoyed her visits to Alicia's salon where she was able to relax for an hour or two away from her studies. Alicia believed in equal rights and opportunity for all people and she and Claire would discuss legal cases and politics and they would weigh in on current and world events while Claire sat in the stylist's chair. Claire admired the warm, well-informed woman who had managed to put herself through hairdressing school, save enough money to open a salon, and raise four children with her loving husband. She'd saved diligently and was able to pay off the mortgage on their home where the family lived in the first floor apartment and rented out the other two apartments in the building. Alicia believed in living within one's means, which was lucky for her family because her husband had suffered a heart attack when Claire was in her second year of law school and the man could no longer work in construction leaving the couple dependent on what Alicia made at the salon and their rental income from the apartments.

Claire joined the long line of people who had come to remember the hard-working woman. The line snaked through the rooms of the funeral home and Claire was glad she had come early because she was certain that in a short time, the line would be outside and around the building. Moving from one room to another, Claire got a peek of Alicia's family standing together greeting the people passing by the closed casket. A short stocky man with gray hair stood uncomfortably shifting from foot to foot and Claire assumed that he was Alicia's husband. Other family members formed a line next to Mr. Fitchburg including adult children and spouses and youngsters that must have been Alicia's grandchildren. Many of them dabbed at their eyes with a tissue and one of the young women openly wept.

Anger bubbled up in Claire's chest as she thought of the person who had robbed years from Alicia's life and who had stolen her away from the people she loved and who loved her in return. A quiet conversation taking place in front of her caused Claire to focus on what the three people who seemed to be clients of Alicia's were discussing.

"The cops better find the monster who did this to Alicia," a woman with short red hair said to her companions.

"She'd been worried about something lately." A short woman with chin-length silver hair touched at the corners of her eyes to brush away tears. "I asked her several times what was bothering her, but she always told me that nothing was bothering her."

A platinum blond spoke keeping her voice so soft that Claire had to strain to hear her. "I was in the salon two weeks ago. A young woman came in and when Alicia saw her, her face changed. She almost looked frightened. She scurried over and stood whispering with the woman for a few minutes. They seemed to be arguing. When Alicia came back to me, her face was pale and she wasn't herself."

"Did she say what they talked about? Did she say what the argument was about?" the redhead asked.

"No. I tried to make light of it by asking if the woman was angry because of a haircut or something, but Alicia didn't even hear what I said. It was very odd. Very unlike her."

Claire leaned forward. "Sorry to interrupt. I was a client of Alicia's years ago. I wasn't eavesdropping, but I overheard your conversation." Claire turned her attention to the blond. "What did the woman look like who seemed to be arguing with Alicia?"

The blond looked surprised by the question and she seemed to be deciding if she should share the information with Claire. "The woman was attractive, looked to be in her early thirties. She had long dark hair, almost black, that fell just below her shoulders. She was dressed professionally in slacks and a suit jacket."

"Had you ever seen her before?"

"I don't recall ever seeing her before that day."

"I wonder who she was." Claire looked across the room. "I wonder what she wanted."

"I wish I knew." The blond pushed at a lock of her hair and then turned back to Claire with wide eyes. "You don't think that woman had something to do with Alicia's murder, do you?"

Claire blinked. "No, no. I was only wondering why Alicia seemed to be so worried after talking with the woman." Even though she denied concerns that the young woman who argued with Alicia in the salon could have had anything to do with the hairstylist's death, Claire couldn't let go of the worry that the visit from the woman could indeed have something to do with the events of the past days.

Two older men came over to join the women in

front of Claire and the discussion of Alicia and the dark-haired visitor to the salon ended. A flurry of unease ran down Claire's back as she thought over what she'd just learned. The description of the visitor sounded very much like Merritt Handley and Claire had a troubling feeling that Merritt was somehow involved.

The idea that Merritt could have had a hand in Alicia's murder caused Claire's heart to race and her stomach muscles to clench. Her thoughts swirled around in her head so fast that she had to shake herself when she discovered that she'd reached the front of the line. Standing in front of the urn that had been placed on a cherrywood table surrounded by flowers, Claire silently recited a prayer and as she turned to offer her condolences to the family members, she made a quiet promise to Alicia Fitchburg. *I will find out who did this to you.*

***

It was dark when Claire and Nicole stepped off the Silver Line bus onto the concourse outside the doors to the domestic departures lobby. Claire was furiously scribbling in a small notebook while Nicole, dragging her carry-on suitcase behind her, jabbered instructions. Nicole's sister had been in a car accident and even though her injuries weren't life-threatening, Nicole was flying to Washington, D.C. to be with her and she'd placed Claire in charge of the chocolate shop.

"Have I told you everything?" Nicole headed for the check-in kiosk.

Claire smiled. "You can always call me, you know. They do have cell service in DC."

"Oh, I know." Nicole removed her boarding pass from the kiosk's metal tray. "I've never been away from the shop. It makes me nervous."

Following Nicole to the security line, Claire reassured her friend. "We'll take good care of everything. The recipes are in the safe and I know my way around a mixing bowl."

Nicole chuckled. "I know you do." She hugged Claire. "Thank you so much. I'll be back in a few days. I don't know what I'd do without you."

"We'll hold down the fort." Claire gave a mock salute. "We won't let you down."

Nicole walked to the security line and into the roped off section to the screening checkpoint. She looked over her shoulder at Claire and mouthed, with a concerned look on her face, *stay safe*.

Claire nodded, waved, and headed to the escalator. She was starving and wanted to stop for a quick bite to eat at one of the fast-food places upstairs before taking public transportation home. She texted Tony to report that she'd be there shortly to pick up the dogs. Tony responded and

Claire smiled when she read his message that he and the Corgis were curled up on the sofa watching a movie together and that she need not rush.

Reaching the upper floor of the airport, Claire walked along near the metal railing of the balcony glancing down to the first floor at the people bustling around from the airline counters to the security lines and she was glad she wasn't the one flying that night. Air travel could be such a hassle, and Claire was feeling exhausted. All she wanted was to fill her grumbling stomach, pick up the dogs, and head home to crawl into bed. She'd have to rise earlier than usual in order to get to the chocolate shop to start the day's prep on her own.

Stifling a yawn, Claire was about to leave the balcony section of the second floor and head to the counters of the food concourse when she stopped in her tracks. She sidled to the wall at the end of the balcony and peered around to look below. On the first floor, standing in a deserted corner behind a closed merchant cart, was Merritt Handley. Merritt, leaning forward, listened intently to a dark-haired young woman standing close to her. In obvious distress, the other woman's cheeks looked flushed and she kept wiping at her eyes with the sleeve of her uniform while shooting glances back over her shoulder. The woman handed something to Merritt that looked like a notebook and Merritt quickly stuffed it into her oversized bag.

Something about the scene caused Claire to feel panicky and beads of sweat rolled down her back. She reached into her small handbag, removed her phone, and not really knowing why she was doing it, lifted the phone slowly to take a photo of Merritt and the woman. Holding the phone tightly in her hand, Claire shuffled backwards away from the balcony and hurried to the food court where she sat down in one of the orange plastic chairs and pulled up the picture she'd taken.

She took a look around to be sure Merritt hadn't come upstairs and then squinted at the photo. Leaning close to the phone screen, Claire used her fingers to enlarge the picture. The face of Merritt's companion was clearly visible in the shot showing the tall, slender woman's facial features and long dark hair covering her shoulders. The young woman looked vaguely familiar to Claire. *Who is she?*

CHAPTER 14

Claire and the Corgis walked into Tony's market and found him in the back store-room taking an inventory of the supplies on the shelf. When Claire had returned from the airport last night and stopped by Tony's to pick up the dogs, the man insisted on walking Claire the few blocks home. When she assured him she would be fine and that she had the dogs for protection, Tony grunted.

"Don't argue with me. It's late and there have been a lot of unpleasant happenings recently and besides, two dogs can't do much against a gun."

Claire wondered what Tony thought he might do against someone with a gun, but his concern for her warmed her heart and she smiled and accepted his insistence to see her safely home.

Taking a seat on a stool, Claire watched the dogs wiggle around Tony as he stooped to pet them and when he straightened, she knew something was wrong.

"What?" Claire eyed the man closely. "What's

wrong?"

"Nothing." Tony turned away to check the items on the shelves.

"What's happened? Tell me." Claire insisted.

Tony removed a few cans and placed them on the counter. "The building has gone up for sale."

Claire cocked her head. "What does it mean?"

"It means that old Tony might get kicked out of the building where he's had his shop for over fifty years." The man's shoulders slumped and worry creased his forehead.

"You don't know that. The new owner would probably be happy to have such a well-established business renting the first floor."

"That's not how it usually works, Blondie."

Claire could see the sadness on the man's face. "Is there a buyer?"

"Not yet."

"Then it will probably take a while for an offer to be accepted and a sale to go through. You have time. You can look around for another building in case the new owner doesn't renew your lease."

"I don't want to move." Tony sat down on a stool across from Claire. "I've been here forever. I'll lose my customer base who also happen to be my friends. I'll probably have to leave my apartment, too. The rents will go up. I can't afford to pay higher rents for my apartment and for space in a new building. I don't get a pension, you know.

I have to be able to fund my retirement once I can't work anymore."

Claire and the dogs visited Tony at least once a day and she didn't want him to have to move out of the neighborhood away from her. She knew that he must be in his mid-seventies and how awful it would be for Tony to leave behind everything he'd worked so hard to build. She let out a sigh wondering why so many things seemed to be so wrong lately. "Wait and see. Maybe no one will buy the building for a long time. Maybe by the time it sells, you'll be ready to stop working."

A hint of a smile played at the corners of Tony's mouth. "You're right. Maybe they won't sell it until I'm six feet under."

Claire's eyes bugged at the man's words. "Don't say that. Don't you dare leave me."

Tony got up and headed for the front of the store. "We all have to say goodbye sometime, Blondie."

"Just don't do it any time soon," Claire scolded and followed him to the front. Pouring a cup of tea, she sat at one of the small café tables squashed into the corner of the crowded store and took out her phone to check for messages. Nothing. She'd sent four texts to Merritt Handley over the course of the day and the young woman hadn't responded. Claire let out a sigh and pushed the phone around on the tabletop in a slow circle, her mind working on the puzzle of why Merritt was at the airport talking to that young woman in what seemed to be a very private and upsetting conversation.

Claire sighed and looked up the phone number of the law firm where Merritt worked. She placed a call.

"Merritt Handley, please," Claire said when the receptionist picked up.

"Ms. Handley is out of the office. Would you like her voicemail?"

"When do you expect her to return?" Claire asked.

"Ms. Handley should be in tomorrow. May I take your name?"

"No, thanks. I'll try again in the morning." Claire clicked off and lay the phone on the table as a cold shiver ran through her body. *Where are you, Merritt? What are you up to?*

Claire pulled the phone closer and as she pushed on the screen, she leaned down to get a better look. She'd brought up the photo of Merritt and the young woman at the airport. She made the photo bigger on the screen and lifted the phone closer to her eyes. Her nose was nearly touching the screen, when Tony walked by.

"You need glasses, Blondie?"

Something on the screen held Claire's attention so strongly that she didn't even hear what Tony had said to her as he passed by. Squinting, Claire was just able to make out the words embroidered on the patch over the pocket of the woman's uniform shirt. *Melody Booker*.

Something pinged in Claire's brain. She searched for the woman's name on social media channels and found her on a professional site listing her as a ground crew operator for Fast Freight Airlines, part of a cargo service that delivered mail, packages, and small freight.

A wave of anxiety washed over Claire with such force that she had to hold on to the sides of her chair for a few moments and suck in some deep breaths. Each time she looked at the woman's picture on her phone screen, the same sensation flooded her body. Claire recalled reading something about Melody Booker, but couldn't remember what it was about. She pushed on the phone screen to close the page and then did an internet search for the woman's address hoping it would be listed. "Bingo."

"Tony, can the dogs stay here for a couple of hours? I need to go meet someone." Claire was already up and carrying her paper cup to the trash bin.

"You bet they can." Tony peeked around from behind a shelf with one eyebrow raised. "Is the man you're meeting good-looking?" he teased.

"It's not a man." Claire hurried out the door of the market and jogged to Beacon Street to flag down a cab that took her to a gritty neighborhood of three-deckers on the outskirts of Boston. Striding down the sidewalk watching for the numbers on the buildings, Claire found the one she wanted and climbed the front porch steps to ring the doorbell. Two big pots of red geraniums stood on each side of the door. A minute passed and no one answered so Claire tried the bell again and got the same result. She pushed on the bell for the first floor apartment and just as she was about to give up, the door opened. A tiny, older woman wearing an apron stood looking at Claire with a questioning expression. "Yes?"

"Sorry to bother, but I'm trying to get in touch with Melody Booker." Claire smiled trying to put the woman at ease. "This is her building, isn't it?"

"She lives upstairs." The older woman wiped her hands on her apron. "But she's probably at work."

"At the airport?"

The woman nodded. "She works different hours, but if she isn't answering her doorbell then she must be at work."

"Do you know Melody well?"

"Not very well. She's a pleasant girl. We chat sometimes. She watered my plants when I went away."

"Have you seen her today?" A growing sense of unease picked at Claire.

"Not today."

"Did you happen to hear her come home last night? I know she was working at the airport last night."

The woman placed her palm against her cheek. "Hmm. I don't think so. I go to bed early. Melody gets home after I go to bed."

"Do you have her telephone number?" Claire felt that something was wrong and a growing sense of desperation flooded her body.

"Oh, I don't know, hon. I don't think Melody would want me to give out her number."

"You know her number, though?"

"I have it in the house."

"Could you call her? Would you call her to see if she's okay?"

The older woman's eyebrows went up. "Why would you think Melody wasn't okay?"

Claire quickly made something up. "I lost her number and I can't reach her. I worried if she got home all right last night."

The older woman stared at Claire for almost a full minute before saying, "I guess I could give her a ring."

"Would you? Thank you so much. When you reach her would you ask if she'd talk to me for a minute?"

"What's your name, dear?"

"Claire. Tell her I'm a friend of Merritt Handley."

The woman hesitated. “I’ll go in and make the call. Why don’t you wait here on the porch? I’ll be back in a minute.”

“I’ll wait right here. Thank you.” Claire smiled at the woman and watched as she closed the door and went inside. Claire heard the door lock. She couldn’t blame the woman for not letting her into the apartment.

Claire paced on the porch and pushed her curls out of her eyes. Her heart was pounding and she wondered what she would say to Melody once the woman made the call. She stopped. *What am I doing? What am I going to say to Melody? Am I losing it?*

The door opened and the woman peeked out. “There wasn’t any answer. Melody must be busy at work.”

Claire’s heart sank. “Okay. Thank you for taking the time.” Walking along the sidewalk, Claire headed for the main street to find a cab to take her home. The feeling that had come over her was stifling and she couldn’t shake it off. *Why won’t Merritt answer my texts?*

Something is terribly wrong.

CHAPTER 15

Riding in the back of the cab, Claire did an internet search on her phone to see if she could find Merritt's address, but as she expected, nothing was listed. Claire thought it would probably be foolish for an attorney to list her address in case a disgruntled client wanted to find her. Letting out a sigh, she watched out the cab window at the people moving about the crowded sidewalks.

Trying to recall why Melody seemed familiar, Claire lifted her phone and did a search on the young woman to see if there was anything of interest about her besides the education and work history that Claire had seen on the professional site. Claire's breath caught in her throat when she saw the articles that came up and her eyes flew over the words on her screen. *How did I miss this? Now I remember.*

News stories reported that six months ago, Melody Booker had applied for a ground crew supervisory position at Fast Freight Airlines, but was not chosen for the position in favor of a young man with less experience at the company. Melody filed a grievance with the airline's union and after an investigation, it was found that the promotion had been inappropriately handled and she was awarded the supervisory position.

Claire had a sinking feeling in her stomach believing that there could have been repercussions against Melody from some angry coworkers who disagreed with the union decision. *Is that why Merritt and Melody were talking at the airport? Is Merritt representing Melody in a harassment suit against the airline? If she was, then why meet at the airport? Why not at the law firm offices?* A pulsing pain had started in Claire's temple and as she rubbed at it with her finger, her phone vibrated with an incoming text. She looked quickly at the screen hoping the text would be from Merritt, but when she saw the name on the incoming call, her mind was blank for a moment until it dawned on her who it was. *Siobhan.* The woman who took the bullet intended for Merritt outside of the Jasper Building. *Can you come to the hospital? I need to talk to you. Now.*

Claire's shaking fingers flew over the screen to send her reply. *I'm on my way.*

***

There were only a few minutes left until visiting hours were over so Claire sprinted from the cab and dashed into the hospital lobby where she caught the elevator and hurried down the hall to Siobhan's room. Siobhan was on the bed resting back against the pillow in the dimly lit room and her face was so pale and still that for a moment Claire thought she might be dead. Siobhan shifted her eyes to Claire and as pushed herself up a little straighter, a flicker of relief passed over the woman's face.

"Thanks for coming."

Claire took a seat near the bed. "Of course. Are you okay? Do you need something?"

"Maybe it's just lying here all day without anything to do."

"What is it?"

"I wanted to tell you something. Something that's been bothering me for quite a while. I haven't breathed a word of it to anyone. Maybe I'm being silly. I don't know."

Claire's forehead creased in confusion and wished that Siobhan would tell her what she was going on about.

"About two weeks ago, maybe it was three weeks ... I heard something at work." Siobhan's eyes darkened and her voice carried a slight tremor. "I heard something that Mr. Freeman was saying." Siobhan made eye contact with Claire. "He was here the other day when you visited, Mr. Freeman, the partner at the firm."

Claire nodded.

"A few weeks ago, I heard him talking on the phone. It was very late. I think Mr. Freeman thought he was alone in the office. I stayed late because one of the other partners needed something done for early the next morning. I walked by Mr. Freeman's office when I went to the other lawyer's office to leave the reports I'd finished for him. Mr. Freeman's door was closed. I paused because I thought he'd left for the day and I wondered who was in his office. I got scared for a moment because I thought I was the only one still working that night." Siobhan's chest was rising and falling quickly. Prone on the hospital bed in the shadowy room attached to a beeping monitor, Siobhan looked frail and small.

"What did you hear?" Claire asked softly.

Siobhan took a deep breath and her shoulders gave an involuntary shudder. "I listened at the door to hear who might be in there and I made out Mr. Freeman's voice. I was about to walk away when I heard something that made me freeze in place. He was angry. He said something like, *I told you to get rid of him. He knows too much. Why is he still walking around?* I nearly choked. He kept talking. He said, *this punk is a loose end. I don't like loose ends. He's not getting in the way of everything we've set up. If he does, you know what will happen to us. Keep emptying those planes. Keep those cards flowing. And get rid of him."*

Claire didn't know what it meant, but she knew it wasn't anything good. "What does it mean? Do you know what he was talking about?"

A few tears gathered in Siobhan's eyes. "I don't know what he means about cards and planes. It sounds like he wants someone killed though."

The same thought had run through Claire's mind, but she thought of something. "If Mr. Freeman is involved with something illegal, he would be smart enough not to be making a call like that using the firm's phone lines."

"He wasn't using the firm's phone. Mr. Freeman has at least three cell phones. One of them looked like one of those prepaid phones. I saw it on his desk. Lots of the attorneys have multiple cell phones, at least one for business and one for personal use. I'm sure Mr. Freeman wasn't using the law firm's phone when I heard him that night."

"Have you ever heard him talking about something that didn't seem above-board before?"

"This was the only time." Siobhan's lower lip trembled. "It sounded bad. I was afraid. I still am."

Claire mulled over what she'd heard trying to make sense of it, trying to think of any legitimate reasons for what Freeman had said over the phone.

"Claire, do you think *I* was the target of the

shooting the other day? Freeman might know that I heard him. Maybe he wants to get rid of me, too."

A cold shudder ran over Claire's skin. "But the target must have been Merritt. Merritt was at both shootings, the one in front of the Old South Meeting House and the one at the Jasper Building.

"Maybe Merritt is in on whatever Mr. Freeman is up to. Maybe they're working together. Maybe they wanted to have me killed, but set up the shooting at the Meeting House first to throw people off. Maybe I'm the target after all."

Claire felt her throat closing up. *Was Merritt working with Freeman? Did they set things up to make it seem like Merritt was the one in danger?* "Did Mr. Freeman see you the night you overheard his conversation?"

"No, I left the building right away."

Claire relaxed a little. "Then I don't think you're in danger. Mr. Freeman would have no idea that you heard him talking on the phone."

Siobhan swallowed hard. "I guess you're right. Being in bed all day messes with my mind." Giving Claire a little smile, she added, "I'm sorry to have been so dramatic. I'm sorry I made you come over here for nothing."

A nurse came into the room to take Siobhan's vitals and she looked at Claire with surprise. "Visiting hours are over. I thought Siobhan was asleep. I didn't know she had company. I'll have to ask you two to say your goodnights."

Claire squeezed Siobhan's hand. "Call me if you need anything."

Siobhan nodded and thanked Claire again.

As Claire was leaving the room, she stopped short and turned back to Siobhan. "Have you mentioned what you just told me to anyone else?"

Siobhan nodded. "Mr. Johnson, one of the other partners. I've always liked him. I think he's a good man."

Oh no. Claire's stomach clenched. "What did Mr. Johnson say about it?'

"He said not to worry. He said Mr. Freeman could be very dramatic at times. Mr. Johnson was sure I misheard or misunderstood. He wasn't concerned at all." Siobhan gave a weak smile. "I guess I let my imagination get the better of me tonight."

Misheard or misunderstood? Claire didn't believe it, not for one second. *Mr. Johnson must have told Freeman about Siobhan's concerns. Freeman knows she heard him.*

CHAPTER 16

Claire left Massachusetts Medical Hospital in Boston's West End and walked along under the streetlamps on the dark streets towards Beacon Hill. Usually, she enjoyed watching the tourists and residents moving about the neighborhoods of the city bustling to their jobs, sightseeing, strolling past stores, or heading to restaurants and bars, but Claire was so deep in thought going over the recent events and happenings that when she was only a few blocks away from Tony's market and apartment building, she wondered how on Earth she'd gotten there so quickly.

Claire wished that Nicole would return from visiting her sister so that she could help sort out the facts and try to make sense of the mess that had gathered around them. Taking out her phone, she texted her friend to ask when she might be returning to Boston and before sliding the phone back into her bag, Claire, her jaw set with annoyance and anger, sent another text to Merritt asking her to get in touch.

Climbing the stairs to Tony's apartment above his market, Claire knocked, entered, and sat down at Tony's kitchen table with her chin in her hand. She spent the next hour telling Tony every single thing that had happened over the past days including her seeing Merritt's and Melody Booker's clandestine meeting at the airport and the visit, an hour ago, to Siobhan Ellis's hospital room.

Tony sat across from Claire with a look that was mixed with equal parts worry, fear, and exhaustion. The two Corgis sat on each side of the man leaning against his legs. "What this is, is a big fat mess."

"You can say that again." Claire's voice was weary. "What do you think is going on?"

"It sounds like this Freeman guy is involved with illegal activity. Either the other lawyer, Johnson, is involved in it, too and is trying to cover things over with Siobhan *or* he really does think that she misunderstood what she heard that night."

"What could the activity be? Freeman mentioned planes and cards."

"Did he say cards or cars?" Tony asked. "Siobhan was listening though a door. The words were probably muffled. Could Freeman be smuggling? He and his companions move things in and out on planes? Transports the goods to and from the planes and the buyers via cars?"

"That's a good idea. You think it's drugs?"

"Likely, I'd say. It could easily be something else, but drugs are the probable choice."

"I wonder if Merritt is involved with whatever Freeman is up to. That could be the reason she isn't friendly with the other lawyers working at the firm. It could be that she wants to keep some distance from everyone so they don't get suspicious about anything." Claire raised an eyebrow. "Siobhan said that Merritt is only friendly with the partners. Convenient, huh?"

Bear and Lady let out low growls.

Claire went on. "And what was that meeting about at the airport between Merritt and Melody?" She rubbed her temple, thinking things over and then her eyes went wide. "Melody works for the airline. She could be working with Merritt and Freeman. Melody could be helping them by getting their contraband on and off the Fast Freight cargo planes."

"Genius." Tony smiled. "But why was Melody crying? And what did she give Merritt? You said it looked like a notebook."

"Maybe Melody is afraid of getting caught. Maybe the notebook has details of what's being moved. Maybe she gave it to Merritt so that police wouldn't find it." Claire stretched her arms over her head trying to get the kinks and tension out of her muscles. "Something about this whole thing is picking at me. Something doesn't add up, but I don't know what it is that I'm missing."

"Do you think that Siobhan should talk to the police about her concerns?" Tony reached down to scratch both dogs' ears.

"I don't think it could hurt, could it?" Claire sucked in a long breath. "Although, if Siobhan talks to the police, they'll start an investigation. That partner that Siobhan revealed her concerns to, Johnson, he'll know she was the one who talked to the police. He'll know that she was the one who brought an investigation on the firm. Could they fire her?"

Tony's face clouded. "Maybe."

"It might be worth taking the chance. Siobhan could be in danger. I think she should talk to the police." Claire eyed Tony's laptop that was pushed to the side of the table. "Can I use your laptop? I'd like to look up Alex Freeman and that other partner, Johnson."

Tony pushed the laptop over to Claire. "Help yourself."

Claire tapped away at the keyboard. "Here's Alex Freeman's biography on the firm's website. He graduated from Yale with a bachelor's degree and then went to law school at Columbia. His specialties are in estate planning, wealth management, and taxes." Claire grunted. "Wealth management, huh? Maybe his own wealth is partially from the movement of illegal drugs."

"Maybe he advises other people in such matters?" Tony raised an eyebrow and frowned.

Claire read more from the internet. "Here are some articles about Freeman attending charity events. Here's a picture of him at a political fundraising thing. I bet he makes big donations and gets some sort of preferential treatment from politicians."

Scanning other articles, Claire read facts out loud to Tony which elicited comments about what a money-bags Freeman was or how he mingled with the social and political elite. "Maybe everybody turns their heads and closes their eyes and lets Freeman get away with his side businesses as long as he keeps things discreet."

"Are all bigwigs involved in things like this?" Claire voice was angry.

"I don't think so," Tony said. "Some are, but it's my hope that most people are honest."

Claire rolled her eyes at the man sitting across from her and returned her focus to the laptop screen where she continued to read about Alex Freeman. After several minutes, Claire let out a gasp of surprise. "Oh, no." She turned the laptop to angle it so that Tony could see what she'd found and she pointed to the line that had caused her reaction.

Tony put on his reading glasses, peered at the words Claire was pointing at, and sat back, blinking. "This isn't good."

"Alex Freeman is on the Board of Directors of the Fast Freight Group." Claire felt sick to her stomach. "Being on the Board would give Freeman access to all kinds of information about the company. He could use that information to benefit his clandestine activities."

"When did Siobhan overhear Freeman's phone conversation?" Tony asked.

"About two weeks ago?" Claire's cheek was pressed against the palm of her hand. "Shortly after she reported what she heard to the other partner, the shootings started. Merritt could be in on this with them. I wonder if Freeman arranged the shootings to make it look like Merritt was the target, when it was Siobhan all along."

"Maybe you should warn Siobhan." The creases on Tony's face seemed to have deepened in the past minute.

"I agree. I'm going to suggest she contact the police. She and I exchanged phone numbers. I'm going to call her right now." Claire checked the time. "If she's asleep and doesn't pick up, I'll leave her a message. It will make me feel better to know I suggested she report all of this to the police."

With shaky fingers, Claire tapped at her phone screen and put the call through. Siobhan didn't answer and her voice mail came on so Claire left a carefully worded message about her worries regarding Alex Freeman and, in light of the shootings, she suggested that the best thing to do would be for Siobhan to share the information with the authorities. When Claire ended the call, a terrible feeling of anxiety flashed through her veins just as Bear let out a loud bark causing her and Tony to nearly jump out of their seats.

Claire looked down at the dog and then slowly raised her eyes to Tony. "Something's wrong," she whispered.

"What do you mean?" Tony's words came out hoarse and he tried to clear the worry from his throat.

"I'm going to call Siobhan's room." Claire found the number of the hospital and placed a call to the woman's room, pacing around Tony's small kitchen while the phone rang and rang. "No one's answering. I'm going to call the nurse's station that's right outside Siobhan's room."

"Why are you so shook up? Siobhan must be dead tired from all she's gone through. She's probably in such a deep sleep that she can't hear the phone at all."

Someone at the nurse's station picked up and Claire said, "Hello, I'm a friend of Siobhan Ellis and I've been calling her room and she won't answer. Can you please check on her for me?"

Claire listened to the voice on the other end, her mouth dropping open, and then she ended the call and turned to Tony with wide eyes. “The nurse told me that she couldn’t release any information about Siobhan. She told me to call the family. Her voice was odd. She sounded uncomfortable.” Claire reached over and squeezed Tony’s arm. “Tony, I think something is very wrong with Siobhan.”

CHAPTER 17

The next morning, Claire arrived at the chocolate shop an hour early to get things ready for the day. When Robby and the two other employees showed up, Claire took off for the hospital to find out how Siobhan was doing. Approaching the room, she could see that it was empty and, sucking in a deep breath, she hurried to the nurse's station to inquire about where the woman had been moved.

One of the nurses stood staring at Claire, her long lashes blinking over her dark brown eyes. "Are you a family member?"

"I'm a friend." Claire knew that she was stretching the truth, but she didn't think she'd get a shred of information if she admitted she was only an acquaintance of Siobhan's. "Has she been moved to another floor?"

"Why don't you call Ms. Ellis's family? I'm sure they'd be happy to share information with you. You understand that we're bound by privacy laws and we're unable to divulge a patient's personal information."

"You aren't allowed to tell me where Siobhan has been moved?"

"I'm sorry." The nurse shook her head and started towards the other end of the long desk. "Talk to the family."

Claire stood by the counter with tension squeezing the back of her neck. She didn't know what to do. The nurses weren't going to give her any information and she didn't know the family so she couldn't call or talk to them about Siobhan's condition. She shuffled a few steps down the hallway feeling miserable and unsettled, unaware that the nurse who was in Siobhan's room last night was heading in her direction.

"Oh, hello." Walking next to a man in a white lab coat, the nurse slowed and nodded as she passed, recognizing Claire from being in Siobhan's room the previous evening when visiting hours were over. "I'm sorry about your friend."

Claire's heart skipped a beat and she could feel her throat constricting. The nurse kept walking and disappeared down the corridor. Claire stumbled, her legs had gone all rubbery and weak, but she caught herself from losing her balance and righted herself. Her only thought was to get out of the building and into the fresh air and sunshine, away from the terrible thing that had happened. Rushing out of the hospital's front entrance, Claire hurried along the walkway to a bench on the green grass in the center of the circular driveway.

Sinking onto the seat, Claire wrapped her arms around herself and rocked gently back and forth trying to calm down. *I just saw Siobhan last night. How could her condition change so swiftly? How could she have died? I was talking to her only a few hours ago.* Claire realized that Siobhan must have been more seriously injured than she'd let on ... still, it seemed beyond comprehension that Siobhan could have taken a fatal turn only a short time after Claire left the hospital last night.

Claire's stomach lurched and she sat stock still on the bench staring vacantly at the traffic rushing by on the busy street in front of the hospital. *Did Siobhan's condition worsen because ... because she had help? Did someone visit Siobhan's room late last night, after I left the building? Did someone kill her?*

Claire glanced around at the well-landscaped grounds feeling light-headed and woozy. *I need help. I need to tell someone my worries. I....*

Reaching into her bag, she took out her wallet and removed a business card she'd put there less than a week ago. *Detective Ian Fuller.* Claire pushed the detective's number into the phone and left him a message.

***

Claire managed to get back to the chocolate shop, but she worked in a daze refusing to answer any of Robby's questions about what was wrong with her which only made him more interested in knowing why she was so distant and preoccupied.

Among the questions Robby peppered Claire with included, "Are you ill? Did something happen to Nicole? Did someone shoot at you again?" – all of which received an answer in the negative leaving Robby stumped about why Claire was acting so oddly.

By early afternoon Claire felt like she'd been awake for days and as she contemplated going home and crawling into bed as soon as they were finished with the day's tasks, the shop door opened and a tall, fit man entered the shop. Claire did a double-take when she realized it was Detective Fuller.

Robby leaned close to Claire and whispered, "Well, well, look who it is."

"Don't say another word," Claire warned. She walked around from behind the counter to join the detective at a table in the corner.

Detective Fuller greeted the young woman warmly and said, "I got your message. I came by as soon as I could."

Claire was so shaken about Siobhan that she forgot to offer the detective a beverage, but Robby remembered what Detective Fuller had the last time he was in the shop and brought a steaming mug over to the table. Although Claire knew the young man was taking the opportunity to try to hear what the conversation was about, she thanked Robby anyway and gave him a look that told him to head back to the counter and stay there.

"What happened? What got you worried?" Detective Fuller scanned Claire's face with his intelligent eyes.

Taking a deep breath, Claire began her tale, reporting everything that Siobhan had revealed to her about Alex Freeman. She moved on to tell what she'd discovered about Freeman being on the Board of Directors of the Fast Freight Group and how being in that position would provide the law firm partner with inside information that could help his illegal activities avoid detection as he used Fast Freight Airlines to move his goods. Claire ended by voicing her concerns about Siobhan's death and her worries that Siobhan may have been the target of the gunman all along, most likely set up by Freeman and his partner, Attorney Johnson, to whom Siobhan had confided what she'd overheard Freeman discussing in a phone conversation late one night.

"When Siobhan talked to Mr. Johnson she thought she was speaking in confidence with someone she trusted. It turns out that Johnson must be involved with Freeman and whatever illegal thing he's got going."

Detective Fuller's face was expressionless as he stared at Claire. "Do you want a job in the police department?"

Claire started to shake her head before realizing that the detective was fooling with her. "Do you think I'm overreacting?"

Detective Fuller said, "It's important to consider every possibility."

"Had you talked to Siobhan Ellis about the shooting?"

"We did."

"Did she tell you about overhearing Attorney Freeman?"

"She didn't, no."

"So was what I told you news or did you already know that Freeman seems to be involved with something illegal?"

"We look into everything we think is necessary."

Claire realized that she was beginning to get gibberish answers from the detective and she also knew that he couldn't share the details of a police investigation, but something started to feel off to her and her guard went up involuntarily.

"Do you think Siobhan was the gunman's real target?" Claire couldn't help asking more questions. She wanted to watch the detective's expression as she interrogated him.

"We'll have to consider that possibility."

"Do you think other people working at the firm could be in on Freeman's side business?" Claire was wondering about Merritt's possible involvement.

"We aren't sure there is a side business."

"Well, what if there is one? Do you think it's just Freeman and Johnson involved or would other people be pulled into it? Generally speaking, of course."

"That's hard to say."

Claire had started the conversation feeling timid, confused, and frightened, but as the discussion went on her emotions had slowly morphed into something else and she was beginning to feel that she wasn't getting any help or reassurance from the detective. Now Claire was feeling slightly defensive and distrustful.

"I'm glad you reported your concerns." Detective Fuller nodded. "Is there anything else to add?"

"I think that's it." Claire folded her hands in her lap. Even if she thought of more to tell, she decided that she would keep her thoughts to herself.

"Tell me, have you shared these worries with anyone else?" The detective made eye contact with Claire.

"No, no one. I thought it best to only share what I heard and what I suspect with law enforcement." Claire was lying. She'd revealed to Tony the details of Freeman's phone conversation that was overheard by Siobhan and she was planning to tell Tony about Siobhan's passing and her suspicion that Freeman might be responsible for the woman's death. She would also tell Nicole everything that was going on, if her friend ever came home.

Claire was suddenly unsure about Detective Fuller and a wall of distrust encircled her like a castle's protective fortifications.

"That's good that you didn't share this information with anyone else," the detective told her. "I have to ask you to continue to keep it in confidence. It's very important that this information be kept quiet."

Claire nodded.

"Are you okay?" Detective Fuller asked.

Claire wondered if, during their conversation, he'd picked up on the change in her demeanor.

"As okay as anyone could be under these unusual circumstances," Claire said. She looked over to the service counter. "I'd better get back to work." As she stood, Claire deliberately extended her hand and Detective Fuller reached across the table and shook.

"Thank you for getting in touch," he said. "Call again if there are any new developments or concerns."

"I will." Claire released the man's hand, but not before gleaning something from the exchange.

Claire sensed that Detective Fuller was holding back. He *did* know about Freeman and Siobhan ... and he knew something about Merritt Handley, too.

And now, Claire wasn't sure she could trust him.

CHAPTER 18

Standing on the busy city sidewalk, Claire stared at the upper floors of the glass and steel Jasper Building. As she took in a long breath and headed for the front doors, the image of Siobhan being shot outside the entrance to the building flashed in her mind. She opened the heavy glass door, walked to the bank of elevators, and rode to the tenth floor. The Freeman and Johnson Associates' suite was exactly what someone would expect from one of the top law firms in the country, gleaming wood, expensive rugs, tasteful artwork on the walls, and attractive, well-dressed, and efficient receptionists at the front desk.

Claire only had to wait for ten minutes to be ushered down a long hallway to Mr. Freeman's corner office which was decorated and furnished in the same style as the reception area, but with an elevated air of refinement, elegance and wealth. Claire was sure that any client who entered the room would feel that this attorney would be able to erase any legal problems from his or her life and that he would safely restore their stability and security.

"Miss Rollins," Freeman was just closing a closet door and he turned with a wide smile and walked across the room to greet Claire. He wore a fitted navy suit and dark blue tie. "How very nice to see you again."

Something about the man made Claire cringe and when she shook his hand, she was too distracted to try and pick up on any vibes she might have felt him giving off. She glanced at the door he had just shut.

Freeman gestured to the chair in front of his massive desk as he returned to his own leather throne. "I'm sure you're aware of the sad news."

Claire nodded and folded her hands in her lap. "Yes. If you don't mind, I'd like to ask you about Siobhan."

Freeman's dark eyebrows lifted in surprise. "How can I help?"

"Siobhan worked here for some time?"

"Yes, she did. She was well-respected, a hard worker, knew her stuff. We'll miss her terribly." Freeman shook his head slowly from side to side.

"Did she work closely with you?"

"Siobhan worked with several of the attorneys."

"Did she have access to any information that might have contributed to her death?"

Freeman's expression was serious. "How do you mean?"

Claire had to choose her words carefully. "A sensitive case? Some information that someone might not have wanted her to know? Anything that might have been dangerous to be involved with?"

Freeman gave a snort. "We aren't the FBI or the CIA. We're just a law firm, Miss Rollins."

"But working at this law firm resulted in her death."

Freeman's forehead creased into furrows and a flash of something passed momentarily over his face. "The firm had nothing to do with her passing."

Claire persisted. "She was shot right outside the front doors to this building. Why would that be? What could have been the cause?"

"An unbalanced person, a disturbed person who got hands on a weapon?" Freeman shrugged a shoulder.

"So you think it was completely random?" Claire leveled her eyes at the man.

"Well, I don't know. Law enforcement is determining the details. They've not shared those particulars with us."

Claire tilted her head in question. "I thought that Siobhan wasn't the target. I thought that someone else was the target and that Siobhan got in the way. Merritt Handley was at the entrance at the same time Siobhan came out."

Freeman blinked and said, "I don't think that theory has been validated. My own suspicions veer towards the idea that it was random in nature."

"Merritt was near the Olde South Meeting House the night that the other shooting took place. If both things are random, then it's quite a coincidence that Merritt was at both shootings."

Freeman's eyes seemed to darken. "What is it you hope to accomplish from your visit here today, Miss Rollins?"

"I'd like to know more about Siobhan's place of employment. I'd like to know if she seemed herself on the days leading up to the shooting. I'd like to know if a legal case or one of your clients might be behind what's been happening." Claire didn't mention that she suspected Freeman himself or one of his flunkies of causing Siobhan's death.

Freeman's intercom buzzed and he excused himself to answer it. When Claire leaned back against her chair trying to gather her thoughts, something about Freeman's office closet picked at her and she glanced over at the door. Freeman's voice pulled Claire's attention back.

"I have a client shortly." Freeman stood and came around the desk. "If there's anything more I can do, please get in touch." He was wearing his fake smile as he gestured to the door. He and Claire headed down the hall to the reception area where he extended his hand. Claire grasped it with purpose and shook. What she felt convinced her of Freeman's involvement.

She watched Freeman stride away to be sure he was out of earshot, before turning and smiling at the receptionist. The young man was in his early twenties and was dressed in what seemed to be the firm's uniform, a tailored navy suit. His hair was cut longer around his brown eyes. "Is there something I can help you with?"

Claire nodded. "Is Merritt Handley in the office? I'd like to pop in and see her for a moment, if I could."

"Can I make an appointment for you to see Attorney Handley?" The young man was about to say more when he looked over Claire's shoulder.

"Still here, Miss Rollins?" Freeman stood right behind Claire.

Claire made sure her voice was easy and bright. "I'd like to say hello to Merritt."

"Oh, we discourage impromptu visits." Freeman shook his head sadly. "It can be disruptive to the work day and...."

"Mr. Freeman, Attorney Handley isn't in today anyway. Remember we discussed it this morning and...."

Freeman cut off the receptionist. "Thank you, Andrew. Why don't you make an appointment for Miss Rollins to come in to see Ms. Handley sometime that's convenient for her?" Freeman nodded, turned abruptly, and hurried down the hall to his office.

Andrew smiled at Claire. "Would you like to arrange an appointment?"

"Yes, please." While Andrew clicked at his keyboard to bring up the online appointment calendar, Claire spoke up.

"What were you going to say about Merritt? Is she not working today?"

Without looking up, Andrew said, "She didn't come in."

"Is she at court?"

Andrew shook his head. "Would next Tuesday morning work for you?"

Claire pushed for information. "I wonder if Merritt is at home today?"

"I'm not sure where Attorney Handley is." Andrew looked up. "What about next Tuesday?"

"Hmmm?" Claire asked. "Oh, never mind the appointment. I'll try and give Merritt a call tomorrow." Smiling warmly at Andrew, Claire decided to question the young receptionist and made up a tale that Merritt was doing some work for her. "Merritt's helping me with some legal questions I have about an estate. She can be hard to get hold of. Sometimes she says she is going to call, but doesn't. Is she always like this?"

"Ms. Handley is a fine attorney. You are in very

good hands."

Claire gave a slight nod realizing that Andrew was well-trained and would not divulge anything negative about the firm's employees. "Did you know Siobhan? Did you have much interaction with her?"

Andrew looked surprised. "She worked down the hall in one of the paralegal offices. We only just exchanged greetings. I didn't know her well."

"I'd recently made her acquaintance. We hit it off right away." Claire lowered her voice. "Did you notice anything unusual on the day of the shooting? Anything unusual on the days leading up to it?"

Andrew's pleasant expression disappeared and his face looked blank. "I didn't, no."

Realizing that the young man wouldn't be providing any information, Claire moved to the glass door that led to the elevator. "Well, thanks."

She stood in front of the elevator doors waiting for them to open when someone walked over and stood next to her. Claire glanced to her left and realized the young woman wanted to say something.

"I heard you asking about Siobhan." The petite blond seemed nervous and spoke in almost a whisper. "Were you a friend of Siobhan's?"

"A recent friend." Claire got an idea. "Siobhan introduced me to Attorney Handley. I was supposed to meet her at her home this afternoon to go over some paperwork with her, but I've lost the address and Merritt isn't answering her phone. I asked Andrew at the reception desk, but he wouldn't help me. Would you happen to know Merritt's address?"

"Oh, sure." The young woman told Claire where Merritt lived. "We often have to deliver papers to the attorneys at their homes. I know where most of them live." The young woman seemed to relax a little.

"Are you a paralegal?"

The girl nodded. "I just got out of school. I'm new. Siobhan didn't mind all of my questions. She was such a nice person. She helped me a lot. I can't believe what happened to her." The young woman brushed at her eyes.

The doors opened and Claire and the young paralegal stepped into the empty elevator. A tear escaped from the girl's eye and traveled down her cheek. "I can't believe she's dead. I was so shocked when she got shot. I went to the hospital to see her, to apologize."

The hairs on Claire's arms stood up. "Why did you need to apologize?"

"The afternoon of the shooting, Attorney Johnson came into Siobhan's office. I was in there with her. He asked if one of us could run out to the pharmacy to pick up a prescription for him. I said I'd do it. He told me which pharmacy it was. As I was heading out, Attorney Johnson said he had something he wanted me to do and he asked Siobhan to go instead."

"You apologized because Siobhan went out to the pharmacy instead of you? It wasn't your fault," Claire said softly trying to reassure the young woman even as alarm bells sounded in her head. "It was just circumstance. What did Attorney Johnson want you to do?"

"He had some briefs for me to file. I hadn't finished what I was supposed to do and he needed it done right away. Siobhan said she'd take care of it, but Attorney Johnson wanted me to do it for experience."

Unease trickled down Claire's back. Was it a set-up to get Siobhan outside at that very moment? "You didn't have anything to do with it. Don't berate yourself. It's not your fault Siobhan was outside when the gunman was there."

"That's what Siobhan told me." The girl's voice was shaky.

"Did Siobhan seem okay that day? Did she seem like herself?"

"I think so. She was always really nice."

"How about the days leading up to the shooting?" Claire noticed the girl wince when she said the word shooting.

"She was normal."

"You didn't see her worried or upset?"

The elevator arrived at the girl's floor and she placed her palm against the door to keep it from closing. "You know, I did see something. A few days before the shooting happened, I saw Siobhan talking to one of the attorneys. The conversation seemed serious. She looked upset when she came into the office to help me with something."

"Did you ask her about it?"

The girl nodded. "She said it was nothing and we got to work. She looked flustered and I noticed her hands seemed shaky, but then she seemed normal after a little while." The girl nodded at the folders in her hands. "I need to deliver these. Nice talking to you."

Before the girl stepped away, Claire asked, "Who was the attorney that Siobhan was having the upsetting conversation with?"

"Attorney Johnson." The girl gave a sad smile and the elevator doors closed.

CHAPTER 19

After her work day ended, Claire received a welcome text from Nicole reporting that her sister was feeling much better so she would be returning home to Boston the day after tomorrow. Claire took the dogs to the Common and feeling too exhausted to run or exercise, she sat on the grass and watched them jump and chase and play with the other dogs. They returned home after an hour and Claire made dinner, cleaned up, and settled at the dining room table with her laptop to do some research.

Questions about what was going on had nagged her throughout the day. She'd called the law firm again and asked to speak with Merritt, but was told that the young lawyer was out of the office and that her return was unscheduled.

Unscheduled? What did that mean? Claire thought that either Merritt had become frightened about working in Freeman's illegal business and had taken off, or Freeman had sent her on a "business" trip and was keeping her whereabouts a secret.

Wanting more information on the players involved in the odd happenings, Claire started with an internet search on Detective Ian Fuller, but found very little information on the man. The law enforcement website had his picture displayed, had a brief bio reporting Fuller's educational and professional experiences, and listed the man's awards, honors, and charitable associations. The biography seemed deliberately vague.

Next, Claire did a search on Merritt Handley and read about her experiences working on several important cases as a prosecutor for the Middlesex County district attorney's office prior to joining Freeman's law firm. Merritt had been at the private law office for about six months and Claire wondered why Merritt had left the DA's office for a private firm and how she ended up working for Freeman and Johnson.

Claire yawned and stretched and got up to make herself a cup of tea before returning to the laptop and deciding to read more about Melody Booker, the Fast Freight Airline employee, who'd met with Merritt at the airport and appeared to be distressed and upset. Tapping at the laptop keys, Claire saw a breaking news story that caused her to nearly topple from the seat.

The news article provided information on a

missing person, Melody Booker. Ms. Booker had not reported to work at the airline since the night Claire saw her at the airport. Melody had gone out later that night to pick up sandwiches for herself and some of her crew, but she never returned to complete her shift and had not been seen or heard from since. Ms. Booker lived alone in an apartment in Quincy and it seemed that Melody had not been in the apartment since she'd gone to work on the day she disappeared.

Her parents, boyfriend, and best friend had texted and called the woman, but she hadn't answered or responded to their messages. Ms. Booker's car had not been seen or found and police were searching for the vehicle in and around Boston. The family reported that Melody had never gone off like this and they feared what might have become of her. Authorities asked people to call, text, or email if they had any information on Melody Booker and to be alert for either the woman or her vehicle.

Claire sat back with her heart pounding like a sledgehammer. Merritt had disappeared, and now, Melody Booker had gone missing. Claire was sure it wasn't a coincidence.

Where were they?

Claire's phone rang making Claire jump and she scrambled to pick it up when she saw Nicole's name on the screen. "Hi, Nic. Are you still planning on coming home the day after tomorrow?"

"Claire."

The tone of her friend's voice made a cold shudder run down Claire's back. "What's wrong?"

"I just got home. I was going to drop my suitcase here and then come to your place to surprise you." Nicole's words had a tremble to them.

"Are you okay?" Claire stood up.

"No, I'm not. Can you come over here? Claire, someone broke into my apartment. Will you come?"

"I'm on my way."

Claire and the dogs took off out the door and practically ran all the way to Nicole's place located above the chocolate shop. Nicole was standing in the hall outside her third floor apartment when Claire and the Corgis rushed up the staircase. Claire hugged her friend and glanced into Nicole's living room through the open front door.

"Were you here when they broke in?"

"No, it was like this when I got back."

The living room desk had its drawers pulled out and the contents dumped on the floor. The same thing had been done to the drawers of the tall armoire. Nothing else in the room looked like it had been touched. The dogs darted about the space sniffing everywhere.

Claire walked slowly around trailing her hand

over the furniture and she knelt down and touched the drawers and the contents that had been spilled onto the floor.

"Do you sense something?" Nicole watched what Claire was doing. "Can you feel anything about what happened here?"

"I'm not sure." Claire stood and walked around the perimeter of the room. "What's missing? What was taken?"

"That's just it." Nicole led the way into the kitchen. "I don't think anything was taken. The drawers have all been emptied and the closets have been rummaged through, but nothing seems to be missing."

The girls moved into the bathroom and then the bedroom. "The TV is still here and even my laptop. I only took my tablet with me. There's even a hundred dollars in cash on the dresser and it's all still there." Nicole turned and stared at Claire. "Why isn't anything missing? It's kind of creepy."

Claire swallowed and sighed. "A lot has happened while you were gone. Let's sit and I'll tell you about it." She gestured around the room at the mess of stuff on the floor. "This ... might have something to do with what's been going on."

It took over an hour for Claire to tell Nicole all the things that had happened from Siobhan believing that Alex Freeman was dealing in something illegal to Siobhan passing away and

Claire suspecting that Freeman had Siobhan killed. She told her friend about Melody Booker and how she'd brought her union in when she was passed over for promotion. "I'm afraid that Freeman and Merritt Handley are using Melody to arrange transport on Fast Freight jets for whatever Freeman is dealing in. And now Melody is missing."

Nicole's mouth had been hanging open for some time. "What a terrible mess. Who is on whose side?"

"I don't know." Claire put her chin in her hand. "And Merritt is nowhere to be found either."

"You think Merritt has Melody?" Nicole asked, her eyes wide.

Claire shrugged. "I have no idea."

"I've been thinking that the shootings were done to get rid of Siobhan because she overheard Freeman talking about his illegal activity, but he wanted to make people think that the target was Merritt."

Nicole asked, "Why would he want people to think Merritt was the target?"

"Because he and his partner could spin it to make it all about some case Merritt handled while working in the DA's office. They could make it seem like someone was angry over a case she was involved with and that someone wanted revenge. All the focus would be on that and no one would look at Freeman and what he's doing. Then

Freeman would get rid of Siobhan before she spilled the beans on him, but make it look like the real target was Merritt and Siobhan just got in the way."

"Is Merritt working with Freeman or is he using her and she doesn't realize it?" Nicole's head was spinning.

"At first, I thought Freeman was using her, but now I'm not sure. Why would Merritt be at the airport talking to Melody if she wasn't working with Freeman?"

Nicole's eyebrows shot up. "Maybe Merritt isn't working with Freeman. Maybe she found out what he's doing. Maybe she talked to Melody about it. Maybe they're trying to figure out a way to bring Freeman down."

"Then why wouldn't they just go to the police and turn him in?" Claire rubbed at her temple.

Excitement caused Nicole's voice to tremble. "They might be trying to gather evidence against Freeman first."

"Then where are they? If they're trying to get evidence, why would they disappear?"

"Oh, no. Do you think Freeman had them killed?" Nicole clutched her hands together.

Claire's face clouded and her voice was soft. "Someone has to stop that man."

The girls sat in silence for a few minutes thinking everything over. The dogs were still padding through the rooms sniffing the drawers that were toppled onto the floor. When the Corgis walked into the kitchen, Nicole glanced at them and leaned forward towards Claire. "So why do you think the break-in here has something to do with Freeman, Merritt, Melody, and Siobhan?"

"Because you and I were at the first shooting. Merritt came to talk to us twice. Freeman saw me visiting Siobhan. The bad guys must think we have some knowledge of what's going on."

"But why would they break into my place?" Nicole's face blanched. "Were they looking for me?"

"You know I told you that when I was watching Melody and Merritt at the airport, Melody passed a book or notebook to Merritt? I think whoever broke in here was looking for that book. Somebody thinks you and I are involved and that we know more than we do. Somebody thinks we're hiding that book. I can feel it all floating on the air." Claire's lips turned down in a frown. "I think the death of my former hairstylist, Alicia Fitchburg, is linked to this whole thing. The women I spoke to at Alicia's wake said someone had come into the salon shortly before Alicia was killed and seemed to be arguing with Alicia. The way the woman described the person made it sound like Merritt Handley."

Nicole said, "But lots of people fit the description."

"I know, but…." Claire hesitated for a moment. "I feel like I need to find out if there's a link between Alicia and what's been going on. I sense something."

"Ugh, what a mess." Nicole groaned and put her hands on the sides of her face. "What are we going to do?"

Claire took in a deep breath and leveled her eyes at her friend. "We're going to figure this out."

Nicole nodded reluctantly. "There's just one thing."

Tilting her head in question, Claire asked, "What's that?"

"I'm not staying alone here until this is over." Nicole smiled. "Want a house guest?"

The two dogs yipped their approval.

Claire looked at the dogs and then returned her friend's smile. "You bet we do."

CHAPTER 20

Once they'd returned to Claire's apartment, the young women and the dogs curled up on Claire's big sofa and talked for another hour before heading to bed. They made the decision that Claire should pay a visit to Alicia Fitchburg's husband to try to find any shred of information that could help to figure out why Alicia was murdered.

In the morning, Claire made a call to Alicia's husband introducing herself and asking if she might drop by to see him briefly that afternoon. She left the chocolate shop shortly after noon carrying a chocolate-caramel cheesecake and headed to Paul Fitchburg's home in a town bordering Boston. Claire admired the overflowing flower pots standing on each step leading up to the big porch.

A short, stocky bald man with soft kind brown eyes answered the door after one ring. "Claire?" The man opened the door wide and welcomed the young woman to his home. "Call me Paul."

Claire followed Paul down the hall across polished wood floors to a large kitchen at the back of the apartment. White cabinets lined the walls, granite covered the countertops, and a small gas fireplace stood in one corner.

"Alicia loved to cook. I do, too. So we renovated and added this kitchen a few years ago." Paul glanced around and his eyes got misty. "Alicia loved this room."

"It's beautiful."

Taking the cheesecake to the refrigerator and thanking Claire for her kindness, Paul gestured to the farm table set next to two big glass doors that led to a deck overlooking the small, nicely-landscaped backyard. He carried two mugs of coffee to the table and sat across from his guest.

"It's nice to meet one of Alicia's clients."

Claire told Paul how while a law school student she'd loved to visit Alicia's salon to chat with the woman while having her hair done. "I always looked forward to it. Alicia was so great to talk to. We got along so well. It was a well-needed break from school and I appreciated Alicia so much."

Paul ran the back of his hand across his eyes and said in a thick voice, "Thanks so much. It's nice to hear." He cleared his throat. "Alicia had a knack. She always made everyone feel good."

Claire shared some fun anecdotes about the hairstylist and Paul chatted about what a wonderful person Alicia was, before Claire gently moved the conversation to an uncomfortable topic. “Are the police making any progress on the investigation into what happened to Alicia?”

Paul grunted and shook his head. “They have nothing new. I don’t think they’ll solve it. Aren’t the first forty-eight to seventy-six hours the most crucial in solving a thing like this? Well, that’s long past. I hate to say it, but I’m not hopeful.” Paul gripped his coffee mug. “How someone can kill a person and get away with it is beyond me.”

Claire murmured agreement. “My friend and I were present at the first shooting that happened in Boston almost two weeks ago. If we hadn’t acted so quickly, we might have been hit by one of the bullets.” Claire looked at Paul. “I have a feeling that the person involved in that shooting and the shooting in front of the Jasper Building may be responsible for what happened to Alicia.”

Paul raised his eyes and didn’t respond for a few moments. “I’ve had the same feeling myself.”

Claire’s eyes widened in surprise. “Was Alicia worried about anything? Was anyone angry with her? Was anything different than usual?”

“I’ve been racking my brain about this.” Paul ran his hand over his bald head. “Alicia was always upbeat, optimistic, had tons of energy. She ran circles around me. Just before she was ... um, killed, she seemed kind of worried or distracted. I asked what was wrong and she said she was feeling a little tired and wondered if she was coming down with a cold. I didn't think that was it, but I didn't nag her."

"Had she mentioned any trouble at work? Any trouble with customers?"

"Nah." Paul shook his head. "Alicia got along with everybody. That wasn't it."

"Was there any trouble with business associates or a professional advisor?" Claire had wondered if Alicia had used the Freeman and Johnson law firm for anything.

"No. Alicia used the same tax guy and accountant and financial advisor for years. They're all practically our friends."

"Did she have anything to do with a law firm called Freeman and Johnson?"

"Sounds familiar." Paul's forehead creased. "We never used a big law firm, though. We have a friend we use whenever we need legal stuff done."

"When I was at the wake, I heard one of the attendees talking about being in the salon. She mentioned that a young woman had come in one day and that Alicia went to speak with her. They seemed to be arguing."

"Arguing? My Alicia and some woman?" Paul's face showed disbelief. "I don't know. Alicia never said anything about such a thing. You sure someone said that?"

"The person described the young woman who was talking to Alicia." Claire reported what the woman had looked like. "Do you know anyone that matches that description?"

Paul's eyes narrowed while he processed the information and then he let out a quick chuckle. "The only one I know who fits that description is a young lady who grew up in the neighborhood. She's a smart cookie. She wouldn't be arguing with Alicia though. That girl loved Alicia. She lost her mom at a young age and her dad worked long hours so she used to hang around here all the time, ate with us, did her homework here. Alicia would take her to the salon some evenings and on Saturdays. The kid loved it. Alicia gave her little jobs to do. She grew up to be a fine young woman. We're proud of her." Paul winked and grinned. "We feel like we had a hand in raising her since she was here all the time. Sometimes I forgot that she wasn't ours."

Claire smiled and marveled at Alicia's and Paul's generosity.

Paul lifted his index finger and gave his hand a slight shake. "You know, that's why that law firm sounded familiar to me. She works there now."

Claire's heart started to race. "She works at Freeman and Johnson?"

"Yup. She's a lawyer. Like I said, she's a smart cookie. She just got the job there a while ago. The name of the firm slipped my mind. Freeman and Johnson, yeah, that's where she's working now."

Claire sucked in a breath. "What's her name?"

"Merritt. Merritt Handley. Alicia was like a second mother to that girl."

Claire's thoughts were spinning so wildly that she thought she might tumble from the chair. Paul noticed the look on her face and asked Claire if she was okay. "You need something? Want some water?"

"I felt dizzy for a second." Claire apologized and then made eye contact with Paul. "So Merritt was like a part of your family?"

"She sure was."

"Do you still see her? Does she come around?"

"She doesn't come around much, usually holidays, at Christmas to say hello, but she saw Alicia pretty often. Alicia would give me the news and the updates about Merritt. Merritt would drop by the salon, sometimes they'd get together for lunch. They kept in touch."

Claire was trying to sort through this new information. "Did you know that Merritt was at the Olde South Meeting House the night of that shooting I told you I was at?"

Paul's face was expressionless and then an eyebrow went up. "Merritt?"

"She was behind me and to my left. She saw me drop to the ground and she did the same realizing that something was wrong."

"Merritt was there?"

Claire nodded. "I wonder if she told your wife about it."

"Alicia didn't say anything to me about it. Merritt's okay, isn't she?"

Claire didn't know where Merritt was or if she was okay or not. "She's fine. At least, she was that night. I haven't seen her." *Not lately anyway.* "Is Merritt's father still living in the neighborhood?" Claire thought it could be helpful to talk to him.

"Her dad passed away a few years ago. Poor kid. No parents, no siblings. I think that's why she kept in contact with Alicia."

A shudder of unease shimmied along Claire's spine.

Paul's face darkened. "You hear about that woman who's missing?"

Claire's heart jumped into her throat. "You mean the woman who disappeared and didn't return to her job at the airport?"

Paul nodded. "She grew up in this neighborhood, too. A cute girl, sweet, nice family. Melody. I always loved that name."

"Did you know her well?"

"The family lived here until Melody was in her early teens. They moved to Medford, got a nice house there. Still live there, I understand." Paul took a swallow of his coffee and set the mug down.

"I haven't got in touch with them since Melody went missing. I've been shook up about Alicia. I was hoping Melody would turn up." He let out a long, low sigh. "What's going on? So many bad things happening. Alicia, Melody."

"Did Melody know Merritt?"

"Oh, sure. The kids in the neighborhood played together."

Claire's throat was so tight that she could barely squeeze the words out. "Were they the same age?"

"Merritt was a couple of years older. It didn't matter. The kids around here would all hang out together, go down to the baseball field, go to the town pool. The kids separated out from each other once they went to high school, but until then, they hung out in a gang. I mean that in a good way. Not a gang like people mean nowadays."

Her head still spinning from what she'd heard from Paul, Claire gave a slight nod and said softly, "It sounds like it was a great place to grow up."

"It was." Paul looked out the window at the green grass and the colorful flowers growing along the fence. "Too many things have changed though. Too many."

CHAPTER 21

With Tony following behind, the two dogs came out of the market's store room with each one chewing on something.

"Did Tony slip you a treat?" Claire asked the Corgis while reaching for more boxes of rice to place on one of the shelves. She gave Tony the eye. "You'll make them fat."

"It was only a small thing." Tony shrugged. "Dogs get hungry."

"You spoil them." Claire finished her task. "Is there anything else I can help with?"

"Let's sit." Tony brought over two bottles of seltzer. "Tell me what you found out."

Claire arrived at Tony's market right after visiting Alicia Fitchburg's husband, Paul, but the market was busy and she needed to talk to Tony privately so they had to wait until the customers cleared out. Talking quickly in case more people came in to pick up some groceries or deli items, Claire reported what Paul had told her about the ties between Alicia and Merritt, and Melody and Merritt.

"It's a small world, isn't it?" Tony crossed his arms over his chest. "So what are those two girls up to? Either they're working together as partners with Freeman in his illegal activities or they're helping each other, maybe gathering information on Freeman and what he's up to." Tony made a face. "Or Merritt has done something to Melody under Freeman's orders."

Claire nodded. "Those are the only three options aren't they? Can you think of anything else?"

"I think that's it." Tony glanced at the door to be sure no one was coming in. "So what's going on? Are Merritt and Melody guilty of working with Freeman or not?"

"Yet to be determined." Claire sighed. "If Merritt was close to Alicia, then I can't believe Merritt was involved with having her killed."

"But," Tony offered, "Freeman might have been angry with Merritt over something and had Alicia killed as a warning to Merritt to shape up. Merritt might have wanted out of whatever is going on so Freeman killed Alicia to keep Merritt in line."

"That's terrible." Claire's eyes misted over and she wiped at them. She stood up and started pacing. "I've been thinking. I need to talk to someone who works at Fast Freight Airlines."

"How are you going to manage that?" Tony

stared at Claire. "And why would that help anything?"

"I read in a follow-up news article that shortly after Melody got refused for that supervisory job, she'd reported some harassment that was going on among some of the employees. A guy who worked there also reported being the victim of harassment from certain individuals which corroborated Melody's complaints. There's another news article that was printed a few months after the decision about the supervisory job was overturned and the position was given to Melody. It says that Melody and some of her colleagues reported that harassment on the job was escalating and that the union was filing grievances with the airline to force them to investigate the harassment claims. I emailed the guy who was quoted in the story and asked him if he'd meet with me because I have some questions about Fast Freight. He responded and asked what I wanted to know. I'm trying to think how to answer him. I'd like to arrange to meet with him tomorrow evening, if he's willing."

It took Tony a few moments to respond. "Is that risky?"

"Why would it be risky?'

"What are you going to ask him about?"

"The harassment. Maybe while we're talking, he'll reveal something else."

"Let the police handle this. Too many things

have gone on. Alicia and Siobhan are dead, maybe because of this Freeman guy trying to protect his operation."

Claire's voice was soft. "I'm sure the police are handling it, but there haven't been any arrests and Siobhan died only a few days after Alicia was killed. Nicole and I were in the line of fire from the gunman in that car. I cared about Alicia, Tony. I feel like I need to do something."

"You *do* need to do something." Tony's voice was stern. "You need to stay alive." He got up and went behind the deli counter.

"I'll be careful. I'm meeting the guy in a public place. We're only going to talk."

"I don't like it," Tony muttered over his shoulder. "I don't like any of this."

The bell above the door tinkled and the dogs rushed over to greet the entering customer. Claire and Tony turned to see Judge Augustus Gunther coming into the market dressed in his usual attire of trousers, starched white shirt, necktie, and suit jacket. "Good afternoon." Augustus took a seat in the corner and Tony hurried to bring the man a mug of coffee.

"What are you two arguing about?" Augustus asked.

Tony and Claire said in unison, "We're not arguing."

"Why would you think that we're arguing?"

Claire sat down across from the judge.

Augustus said calmly, "I don't *think* you were arguing, I *know* that you were arguing."

"But we weren't." Claire smiled at the man.

Augustus folded his hands and set them on the table. "My dear, I was a lawyer and a judge for over sixty years. I don't need to hear words being uttered, I am able to read body language, I can sense tension in the air."

Claire gave in with a shrug. "It was just a little bickering."

"About those girls?" Augustus asked.

Claire's jaw dropped and Tony stared wide-eyed at the judge.

"What girls?" Claire asked.

Looking from Claire to Tony, Augustus let out a small sigh. "The two of you are not that subtle, you know. I hear parts of your conversations. I read the news. It isn't that hard to put two and two together." Augustus let his words sink in and then he added, "I have experience in legal matters. I know some members of the police force." Augustus's eyes bored into Claire's. "I am acquainted with *other* kinds of people, as well. Should you ever want my opinion or suggestions, I would be happy to listen." He raised his mug and sipped.

Claire leaned forward. "Do you know a lawyer by the name of Alex Freeman?"

Augustus's right eyebrow raised slightly. "Is Freeman involved with the missing girl?"

"I don't know," Claire said, and then she told the judge what she *did* know.

Augustus took in a long breath. "Alex Freeman is an arrogant, small-minded, unethical, sleazy piece of work who should have been disbarred years ago. The man is dangerous, as you have learned. I would like nothing more than for someone to bring Freeman down. Some of us have recently suspected that Attorney Freeman has a side business that takes a good deal of his time ... and is *quite* profitable. I won't say what is suspected because of ongoing law enforcement investigations, but anything that you can find out about him would be worthwhile."

"Hold on," Tony had been waiting on customers as Claire spoke quietly with Augustus about her ideas. Tony came from behind the deli counter. "If this man is so dangerous, I don't think Claire should be pushing her nose anywhere around him."

Augustus narrowed his eyes. "Claire is gathering information. She is not going to accuse Mr. Freeman. She hopes to meet the man who works for Fast Freight to discuss his experiences with harassment in the workplace." Augustus gave Claire a pointed look. "Perhaps Claire is considering applying for a position at Fast Freight. Perhaps Claire has read about the problems at the company and wishes to get the opinion of a current employee. Use that as your reason for contacting the man. Tell him you're thinking of working there. Tell him you saw his name in a news article. Meet publicly. Should you feel uncomfortable at any time, leave. Be aware of who is around, who might be showing interest in your conversation. Keep your voice down." Augustus pointed to Claire's long, wavy blond hair. "Be subtle. Put your hair up. Dress conservatively. Don't call attention to yourself."

Claire nodded.

"If anything is amiss, call my number." Augustus exchanged numbers with Claire.

"I don't like this," Tony growled. "You're both acting like spies or something."

Augustus looked up at Tony who was standing next to the deli case with his hands on his hips. The judge used a gentle tone of voice when he said, "Sometimes there is danger in working against wrong-doers. Claire and I are using our skills for good."

The Corgis woofed in agreement.

Augustus narrowed his eyes at Tony. "Why are you so out of sorts? What's going on with you?"

"Has something happened?" Claire looked at Tony with alarm realizing what might be bothering him. "Is there news about the sale of this building?"

Tony shifted his gaze to the floor. "The current owner called me today. He is entertaining a very good offer. Since I've been a tenant for so long, he wanted me to know."

"He got an offer already?" Claire's voice went up an octave.

Tony cleared his throat. "If the deal goes through, the new owner is planning to turn the building into condos. I'll have to vacate."

Nobody said anything for almost a full minute.

Claire broke the silence. "Maybe it won't go through or if it does, maybe there's a nice place nearby you can move to."

Tony shook his head. "I've been talking to a real estate agent. There isn't anything available in the neighborhood. Anything available in the Back Bay is too expensive for me. It's not looking good. I don't know what I'm going to do." Tony rubbed at his eyes.

Bear and Lady scurried over to Tony and leaned against his legs.

Claire stood up, wrapped her arms around the big man, and said softly, "Don't give up. Things look gloomy right now, but good fortune must be just around the corner."

It has to be.

CHAPTER 22

Claire, wearing black slacks and a light blue button-down shirt, had her hair pulled back and wrapped into a bun to be as plain and inconspicuous as possible. She entered the Back Bay coffee shop and glanced around to see a small, wiry, dark-haired man stand up and make eye contact with her. She gave a nod and headed to the booth at the back of the room where she introduced herself to the Fast Freight employee.

"Joe Elliot." The guy fidgeted in his seat and held tight to his coffee mug.

"Thanks for meeting me." The waitress came over and Claire ordered some tea. She waited for the woman to walk away from the table before speaking. "I've read a lot about Fast Freight. I was thinking of applying there, but the news articles have made me think twice. It would be a big help to me if you could talk a little about the working conditions, especially for women."

The man was muscular and tanned and Claire

guessed he might be in his mid-thirties despite the deep creases in his face.

“I’ve been working there since I graduated high school. I started the very next day. The pay is good, they offer a pension, give three weeks of vacation, health insurance. A lot of people would like to get in there.” Joe hesitated and then said, “But things have changed since I started.”

“How have things changed?” Claire asked.

“Used to be a friendly place, everybody got along. We worked hard, but we’d have a good time. The shift would fly by.”

“And now?”

“You read about the harassment? Things changed about a year ago. Some new guys started. They can be hard to work with.”

Claire waited for the man to go on with the story.

“One guy in particular. He causes trouble. We have a break room. It can get uncomfortable in there. These new guys talk dirty. I’m no prude, I do my share of swearing, but these guys ... I don’t know.” Joe shook his head. “The things they say are over the top. We got women working the ground crew, they work hard, they pull their weight. Most of us got nothing against them, we work together good. We get along good. But these guys, they say dirty stuff, it makes all of us uncomfortable. If you say anything or act uncomfortable, then they go after you. They push people around, do nasty things to people's lunches. They hang up dirty pictures on the fridge. It's sick."

Claire could see the tension building in the man as he reported on the workplace environment.

"Some of the things they do seem illegal."

Claire's eyebrows went up.

Joe went on. "The girl they mentioned in the news article, Melody Booker? She was taking the brunt of things since she filed that grievance about the promotion. She should of gotten that job right off the bat, but management gave it to the guy who applied. He hadn't even been there half the time Melody has been there. Some of the guys used to harass Melody before, but she got it good after the job was finally given to her."

"What happened?"

"They drew naked pictures of her and hung them all over the place. Wrote rude comments. They'd push her around, push her into a corner and whisper things to her. The worst thing was right before she went missing. They drew a picture of a coffin with her in it and wrote something like, *your time is up*."

Claire swallowed hard and lowered her voice. "Do you think those guys did something to her?"

Joe's eyes darted around the coffee shop. "I don't know." He looked like he wanted to bolt, so Claire didn't ask any more questions about Melody's disappearance. "Do they harass some of the other women?"

"Sure, they even do stuff to some of the men, me included. Melody gets it the worst though."

"Why do you think she does?"

"She's a pretty girl. I think they resent a woman doing the job. Melody has some ambition. She wants to do as well as she can. She doesn't bend the rules. The guys don't like that. They don't like having a woman as a supervisor."

"Those guys ask Melody to bend the rules?"

Joe nodded. "That's what she told me."

"What do they want her to do?"

Joe shifted around uncomfortably in his seat and avoided making eye contact.

Claire asked again. "Did Melody tell you how they wanted her to bend the rules?"

Giving a shrug, Joe looked up. "I don't trust those guys. They're bad news." Joe seemed to be struggling with how much he wanted to tell Claire.

"Do you think those guys are up to something?" Claire asked, her voice just above a whisper.

Joe's eyes widened and he pushed against the chair back, blinking. "What do you mean?"

"Could they be doing something illegal when they're on the job?"

Joe's lips held tight together in a thin line and the muscle in his jaw twitched. "Why do you say that?"

"I've read the articles about the harassment. I

have a feeling that those guys are doing something illegal. Maybe loading or unloading things from the company jets? I wonder if it could be an organized ring, well-run and efficient. They probably want a supervisor they can push around so they can remove things from the jets without interference."

Joe looked like his face had gone all rubbery. He grabbed his mug and drank the remaining liquid in one big swallow. When he placed the mug on the table, his face was flushed. "I ain't saying anything about that."

"Were you working on the day Melody went missing?"

"I didn't do anything to her, if that's what you might be thinking." Joe's voice shot up in pitch. "She was my friend. I'm not part of whatever the guys are up to. Are you an investigator or something?"

Claire shook her head. "Absolutely not. And I don't want a job at Fast Freight. I want to know what happened to Melody. I think two people have been killed because of what's going on with Fast Freight. I want to know who killed them. And I want whoever is responsible for their deaths to be brought to justice."

Joe's shoulders seemed to relax a little. He nodded. "The night Melody went missing, she asked the crew if they wanted to order from the sandwich shop. She wrote everything down and called it in. She left to go pick up the food." Joe's eyes glistened. "I asked her if she wanted company, but she said no. I should have gone with her anyway."

Claire asked gently, "How did Melody seem that day? Was she herself?"

Joe turned his empty mug in small circles on the tabletop. "Melody was always positive. She was strong. She knew what was right and wrong. She was funny, good to work with. She was quiet that night, didn't really seem like herself. I wondered if she was coming down with a cold or something."

"Did you see those guys harassing Melody that night?"

"No, I was working a different ramp. A guy called in sick so I was covering for him. I didn't see Melody until we were in the break room." An angry expression washed over Joe's face. "There was another picture on the fridge. It was a drawing of a cemetery. There was a grave and a headstone. It said "Melody Booker" on the headstone. I ripped it off the fridge and stuffed it in the trash." Joe balled his hands into fists. "I'd like to do the same to the person who drew that thing."

"What happened when Melody didn't come back to work with the food?"

"A couple of us kept checking the clock. We were all working on the ramps. I texted her a couple times. No answer. Remember I said I wondered if she was coming down with something? I thought maybe she got worse and just went home."

"I read that someone clocked her out that night when the shift ended."

Joe gave a nod. "Some of us were afraid that Melody would get into trouble for not coming back to finish the shift. Maybe somebody clocked her out to cover for her."

"Did you notice if any of those guys who bother Melody had gone out around the same time she left on her way to pick up the food?" Claire asked.

Joe's forehead creased in thought. "You know, I didn't think anything of it at the time, but I was in the break room hoping that any minute Melody would come in with the food. The jerk came in and I turned to leave. He grabbed me and tried to push my head into the trash can. He said, *waiting for your food? Maybe you'll go hungry tonight.* Someone else came in and pushed the guy off me. We got out of there fast." Joe's face seemed to blanch. "My God. You think he did something to Melody?"

"Did you tell the police what he did to you? Did you tell them what he said?"

"I just remembered it now. Should I tell them?" There was a touch of panic in Joe's voice.

"I think you should." Claire held the man's eyes. "Don't tell them I talked to you though, okay? Just tell them you remembered something. Tell them about the cemetery drawing, too."

"I will." Joe ran his hand over the top of his head. "Why didn't I think of this before?"

Claire glanced around and lowered her voice. "What did Melody tell you about those guys wanting her to bend the rules?"

Joe swallowed hard. "You know what? I'm afraid of those guys. I'm not going to say much. Don't tell anyone what I'm about to tell you. I'll just deny it." He sucked in a deep breath. "When jets were due to land, those guys would go into Melody's office, it was the size of a broom closet, and they'd use the computer in there to look stuff up about the incoming plane. Melody and I think they stole her keys and had a set made so they could get in there whenever they wanted. We had no idea what they were trying to find out. Melody and I, we both heard them say something about the weight of the cargo, but we didn't know what it meant to them."

"Did those guys unload the jets?"

Joe nodded. "Sometimes they forced a crew to trade planes with them. There was something they wanted from some incoming planes and when that was the case, they made the other crew switch ramps so they could get into the planes they wanted."

"Did you ever see them take things from the planes?"

“No, that’s what’s so weird.” Joe shrugged. “It seemed like normal cargo. What were they doing?”

“Did you ever see them load things onto planes? Things that were unscheduled?”

“No, never.”

Claire took out her phone and turned the screen to Joe so that he could see the picture on it. “Have you ever seen this woman? Have you ever seen her with Melody?”

Joe took the phone and brought the screen closer to his eyes and his face showed recognition. “Yeah. Yeah, I saw her. I saw her talking to Melody. They were off in a corner of the airport. It was the night Melody went missing. I was walking in to start my shift. I remember because they seemed to be having a serious conversation.” Joe handed the phone back. “I also remember because I thought that woman was a looker. Who is she?”

Claire fibbed. “I don’t know. She’s been seen with Melody.”

Joe checked his watch. “I better get going. I need to get to the airport.”

Claire thanked the man for meeting with her. “Joe, what’s the guy’s name who told you that you might not be getting your food that night, the guy who was harassing Melody?”

Joe’s eyes darted around the coffee shop. Before he stood up, he leaned forward. “Mickey Sleeper. He’s like the ring leader. His brother is one of the other trouble makers, Joel Sleeper. The guy's as dumb as a stone." Joe tossed some money on the table and got up. "Those two are as mean as rattlesnakes. They got no conscience, got no morals. Their flunkies do whatever Mickey and Joel tell them to do." Joe looked Claire in the eye. "Whatever you do, be careful."

A shudder of anxiety zipped down Claire's back as fast as Joe hurried out of the coffee shop.

CHAPTER 23

Claire and Nicole sat at the patio table in the dark under the tiny twinkling lights that Claire had strung between the two garden trees eating pasta, green salad, and Italian bread. The dogs lounged in the grass near the fence snoozing in the cool evening air. Claire had just finished telling Nicole about her meeting with Joe Elliott, the Fast Freight employee and colleague of Melody Booker.

Nicole dipped a piece of her bread into some oil. "The biggest question I have, other than what are those guys doing with some of the arriving planes, is what's going on between Melody and Merritt?"

"That's been my biggest concern as well." Claire added some grated cheese to her pasta. "I've been trying to figure out if Merritt is working within the ring or not. Is she working with Attorney Freeman or is she working against him? Could she have helped Melody disappear or did she cause Melody's disappearance?"

"Which way are you leaning?" Nicole asked.

Claire looked up at her friend. “I’d like to hear what you think first, then I’ll tell you my thoughts. I don’t want to influence you one way or the other.”

Nicole drew in a long breath and set her fork down on her plate. “From everything I’ve heard, I’m inclined to believe that Melody and Merritt are working together, on the outside. They’re not involved with the illegal activity.”

“Why do you think so?” Claire was trying to organize her own thoughts and wanted to hear the reasons why Nicole believed that the two women weren’t working within the illegal ring.

“Well, they knew each other as kids and probably still have some level of fondness for one another. Melody has been having problems at work so that suggests that she isn’t cooperating with those involved with the crime ring. The harassment, being initially passed over for the promotion, the drawings and threats all seem to indicate that she is on the outside of the gang. “Gang” probably isn’t the right word, but I don’t know what else to call them.” Nicole went on. “Merritt seems to have done very well prosecuting cases when she worked in the DA’s office so she is obviously smart and hardworking. When she joined Freeman’s law firm, she might have overheard things about Fast Freight that made her suspicious. Maybe after hearing about or reading about Melody’s harassment in the news, Merritt got in touch with her. Merritt might have suspected that Attorney Freeman is running some illegal thing at Fast Freight and decided to ask Melody if she knew anything about it."

A little smile spread over Claire's lips. "I'm relieved to hear you say all of that. It's the same way I've been leaning. I wasn't sure if I was being logical about it or if I was leaning that way because it's what I hope is true. I'm glad you feel the same."

"I think it makes the most sense." Nicole sipped from her glass of water. "Of course, we could come up with a plausible scenario placing both women in the middle of the crime ring, but I just don't get the feeling that they're involved with it."

"I agree." Claire gave a nod. "I think that Merritt is trying to help Melody. I think she's caught up in the mess by chance."

Bear and Lady both let out a woof.

Claire and Nicole laughed and the dogs went over to the table to cajole the young women into patting them.

Rubbing under Lady's chin, Claire felt a wave of unease pass over her as she thought about what she wanted to talk about next. "We need to focus on where Melody and Merritt could be. Have they been hurt? Have those Fast Freight guys put their threats into action? Have they kidnapped Melody and Merritt?" Claire's voice went soft. "Have they killed them?"

Nicole shuddered. “I can’t even let that thought enter my head. When it tries to weasel its way in, I push it down and focus on something else.”

“If those guys have them, I don’t have any idea where to look. But....”

Nicole cocked her head. “But, what?”

Claire’s face was serious. “But what if they’re together, hiding out?”

“It’s possible. They might have gotten wind of something about to happen and they took off.”

“I’ve been wondering.” Claire ran her hand through her curls. “They couldn’t hide out in a hotel. These guys seem sophisticated. I wouldn’t be surprised if they had someone who could track credit cards. They certainly wouldn’t hide out in their apartments.”

“They might be with friends or family,” Nicole offered.

“I think Merritt would think that was too dangerous. If they were found, then that would put whoever they were staying with at risk.”

“Do you have an idea?” Nicole stared across the table at Claire.

“I’ve been wondering if one of them has a cottage or a cabin somewhere. Merritt might have inherited a place or maybe Melody’s family has a house somewhere.”

“They could be hiding out there.” Nicole gave a nod. “That’s a good idea.”

"I think we should try to find them."

Nicole sat up straight. "Why? Isn't it better to leave them alone? We could end up drawing attention to them."

"I think we need to talk to them, find out what they know. Bring the information to the police."

"That brings up another question." Nicole leaned her elbow on the table. "Why haven't Melody and Merritt gone to the police?"

Claire ran her hand over Lady's soft fur. "I wonder if they have. Melody brought the workplace harassment to light. She got her union involved. Maybe the police investigated? Maybe they are still investigating?"

"Did the guy you talked to today, Joe, did he say anything at all about the police asking questions at Fast Freight?"

Claire shook her head.

"Maybe the police aren't involved then." Nicole frowned.

"Could Melody or Merritt have alerted the police to what they knew, but...."

"But what?" Nicole's eyes darkened.

"If this is a big crime ring, could some police officers be on the payroll? Could they brush complaints under the rug to keep the operation running?"

Nicole visibly shuddered. "Ugh. This could be a bigger mess than we thought. If there are police officers involved, then the guilty parties may never be brought to justice."

Claire's face clouded. "I can't believe that would happen."

Nicole eyed Claire. "Do you get any *feelings* about what's going on?"

"My thoughts are so jumbled that I don't know what I think or feel anymore. I don't know how to sift the *sensations* from my normal thinking." Claire rubbed her temple. "I do know one thing though. I feel like I'm failing them."

Nicole was just about to say something when Claire's phone dinged with an incoming text. Leaning forward to see who had sent the message, Claire jumped from her chair. "Nicole," Claire's voice was breathless. She pushed the phone across the table so Nicole could read it.

I need help. It was from Merritt.

With shaking fingers, Nicole lifted the phone from the tabletop. She raised her eyes from the screen and looked at Claire. "Answer her." She passed the phone to her friend.

Where are you? What do you need? Claire pushed the send button.

Standing by the table, they waited for a response. Claire's heart pounded like a drum.

"Why won't she answer?" Nicole asked.

The phone dinged.

I'm shot. Can't get out on my own. 136 Weston

Avenue. North End. Hurry.

“She says she’s been shot. She sent an address.” Claire’s breath was quick and shallow.

Nicole pulled up a map of Boston on her phone and zoomed onto the address that was sent by Merritt. “It’s right here, near the waterfront. Looks isolated, like a bunch of warehouses.” Nicole made eye contact with Claire. “Let’s go. We can get a cab. Grab your pepper spray. I’ll get a knife from the kitchen drawer.”

“Should we call the police?” Claire hurried into the house from the patio with Nicole and the dogs rushing after her.

“I don’t think so. Not yet. Let’s wait until we get there.” Nicole removed two knives from the kitchen drawer.

The two young women darted about grabbing the things they needed.

“Bring the dogs,” Nicole said as they raced to the front door.

Just as Nicole put her hand on the doorknob, Claire reached out and grabbed Nicole’s arm to stop her. She raised her index finger to her lips and then took the knob in her own hand. Trying to breathe deeply in and out, she held the knob for a few moments, and then Claire slowly turned her head to Nicole and whispered, “Something’s not right.” She gestured to the back of the house and the women and the dogs walked briskly, but quietly down the hall.

Claire pushed open the sliding glass door to the back garden and waved for Nicole to follow. Once outside, Claire spoke in a soft voice. “Something’s wrong. I got a bad feeling when we were about to go out the front door. Let’s go this way.” Claire pointed to the fence.

“Climb over?” Nicole looked through the darkness at the fence as Claire walked to the corner, tugged on a loose board, and yanked it to the side. Squeezing through, she waved for Nicole to do the same and once her friend and the dogs had slipped through the opening, Claire pushed the slats back into place.

They hustled along the fence and through the neighbor’s yard to the quiet neighborhood that led around to the upper part of Claire’s street. Walking softly through the dark alley between two brick townhouses, they hugged the shadows and peered around to the front of Claire’s building.

A dark sedan was parked at the curb. In the glint of the streetlamp, behind the lowered back window of the car, Claire could make out the muzzle of a gun pointing directly at her front door, waiting.

CHAPTER 24

Claire stifled a gasp and pressed her back against the brick wall. The dogs looked up at her with alarm, but they kept silent while Nicole moved closer with a concerned expression on her face. She mouthed, *what is it*?

Claire pointed to where they'd come from and they inched back and around the building to the narrow alley. The dogs sat at Claire's feet watching their owner try to slow her breathing. "That car in front of my house." Her words were ragged with fear. "Someone was in the backseat. He had a gun."

Nicole's eyes went wide. "A gun?"

"It was trained on the front door. They were waiting for us to come out. They would have mowed us down." Tears glistened in Claire's eyes.

"You felt it." Nicole whispered and squeezed Claire's arm. "You saved us."

"We need to get out of here." Claire looked down the alley. "What will they do if we don't come out of the house? Will they break in or start searching the streets?"

"Maybe both." Nicole grabbed Claire's wrist and pulled her further down the alley. "They aren't going to wait long before they do something. Let's get out of the neighborhood."

Claire signaled to the Corgis to be silent and the four scurried down alleys and streets and ran to the river to cross over the bridge into Cambridge. They slumped down behind some trees next to a deserted playground to catch their breaths and figure out what to do. "We need to turn off our phones. They might have some way to use them to track us."

"Really? God." Nicole shut her phone down.

"They must know that I talked to Joe Elliott. They're worried about what he said to me." Claire's face blanched. "Oh, no. I need to contact Joe and tell him what just happened. He might be in danger for talking to me." Claire pulled out her phone, turned it back on, and placed a call to Joe. "He isn't answering." She left him a message telling what had just happened and warned him to get out of or stay away from his house. "I'm calling "911" to report the gunman outside of my house." Claire made the call, explained what happened, described the car as best she could while cursing herself for not getting the license number, and asked the dispatcher to send a patrol car to Joe Elliott's house in Quincy to be sure he was safe. When the dispatcher asked Claire where she was, Claire thanked the person, hung up, and immediately turned off her phone.

"What about Merritt?" Nicole asked. "Should we go to her?"

"I think those men have Merritt's phone. I think *they* sent me the text message that she needed help, it wasn't from Merritt." Claire leaned her head back against the tree trunk. "It was a ploy to get me outside ... so they could kill me."

"What are we going to do?" Nicole looked out across the dark Charles River. "We can't sit here all night."

"You could probably go home. They know you didn't talk to Joe Elliott. You're probably safe."

"No, thanks." Nicole eyed Claire. "I'm not taking the chance. And I'm not leaving you, so think of something else."

"I'm coming up empty here," Claire practically whimpered as she pulled her knees up to her chest, put her arms on them, and rested her head against her forearms. Bear got up and walked over to his owner. He slurped his tongue over her cheek.

Claire lifted her head and hugged the dog.

"Bear says you better not be giving up," Nicole said. "We all need you."

Claire gave a shrug and was about to speak when Nicole cut her off. "Lay back on the ground. Close your eyes. Open yourself to whatever it is in the universe that tells you stuff."

The corners of Claire's mouth turned up at Nicole's description.

"Do it, Claire. Get us out of this mess."

Claire sucked in a long, deep breath, hesitated for a moment, then rested back on the damp grass and closed her eyes. At first nothing happened, but then, Claire felt like she was in a dream state even though she knew she was fully conscious. Her muscles relaxed and her breathing evened out and became slow and easy. Images popped into her brain of the things that had happened recently, beginning with the night she and Nicole experienced the shooting by the Old South Meeting House. She saw Merritt outside the Jasper Building and Siobhan getting shot. As one image faded, a new one came together like snippets of video, one after another.

A vision of someone took form in her mind ... a small, skinny man dressed in black, approaching Siobhan in her hospital bed with a hypodermic needle in his hand. Just as he plunged the needle into Siobhan's arm, the picture dissipated and Claire saw three men in a tiny room hunched over a computer checking the weight of the cargo being carried in the hold of the incoming jet. She saw the smiles on their faces when they realized that what they were waiting for was on the arriving plane.

Her visions went black and Claire thought it was

over until she saw tiny sparkles at the edge of her vision swirl around until the blackness was gone. A man, dressed in a suit, sat at a large wooden desk in front of a huge window in a beautifully furnished room. He tapped at a laptop and his gaze on the screen was intense. It was Attorney Freeman. There was a desktop computer on his desk and he had a second laptop on the corner of his workspace that was closed.

When he finished what he was doing, he shut down the laptop, stood, and carried it across the room where he opened a closet door. He punched a code into a keypad on the wall, swung a metal door open, and slid the laptop inside of the safe. He exited the room leaving the other laptop in plain view on his desk.

Claire bolted upright. "The safe."

Nicole stared at her like she'd lost her mind.

"Freeman put a laptop in his safe." Claire stood. "He locked it in his safe. That laptop must have information on it about his illegal activity. That's why he's hiding it in his safe."

Nicole jumped to her feet, her mouth hanging open. "You *saw* that?"

"Don't look at me like that." Claire held out her hand. "I need to use your phone. It's probably safer than using mine. Then we're getting out of here."

Nicole handed the phone to her friend.

Claire said, "I'm calling in some help."

***

Despite the late hour, Claire made her second call of the day to Judge Augustus Gunther to report the evening's activities. She'd spoken to the judge earlier in the day right after she'd met with Joe Elliott to tell him what she'd learned about Fast Freight and the harassment that was going on there. After Claire told Augustus about the car in front of her house and the supposed text from Merritt, she spoke to him about Alex Freeman's laptop ensconced in a closet safe in the man's office and what she suspected could be found on that laptop. "I can't reveal how I discovered this, but I know he keeps a laptop in his office safe."

It took so long for Augustus to respond that Claire thought the phone had gone dead. At last he said, "This is very useful. I must consider how to proceed."

"I don't know who to trust," Claire told the judge. "I thought you would be better equipped than me to know what to do with this information and who to share it with."

Claire listened to Augustus for another minute and then ended the call.

Handing the phone to Nicole, Claire said, "Let's go back to the house."

Apprehension washed over Nicole's face. "The house? We can't. Why go back?"

"Because it's more comfortable than sitting on the cool, wet grass of this playground." Claire started walking.

"What about the car in front of the house? What about the gun?"

"I called it in to the police. That car isn't going to sit out there all night. Anyway, I need to get home. There's something I have to do."

The two Corgis trotted ahead as Nicole hurried along beside Claire. "Do you want to share with me what it is you have to do?"

Claire gave a wan smile. "I will. I just don't know what it is yet."

CHAPTER 25

When Claire, Nicole, and the dogs arrived home to the townhouse, Detective Fuller and two plainclothes police officers had just walked the periphery of the property and were about to contact the building manager to open the apartment. When Detective Fuller saw the women and dogs approaching the house, a look of relief washed over his face.

Sitting in Claire's living room, the girls explained the evening's events to the detective while the officers searched the house. Claire talked about the panic she felt when she saw the man with a gun sitting in the parked car outside the townhouse.

After an hour of questions, Detective Fuller told Claire and Nicole that the two men from the vehicle had been apprehended and taken in for questioning. Because of Claire's emergency call to the police, it was discovered that Joe Ellis had been at a family member's birthday party and was safe. A police car would be stationed in front of the townhouse for the rest of the night while law enforcement assessed the situation.

After the detective and the officers left the townhouse, the girls retired to their beds, but neither of them slept a wink.

The next morning, Nicole, Claire, and Robby bustled about the chocolate shop getting ready for the morning rush. The girls were unusually quiet while they worked and Robby kept pressing them for the reason for their subdued manner. “You’re like a buzzing mosquito,” Claire grumped which only served to make Robby more interested to discover why the young women were in such foul moods. “Did you get shot at again or something,” he joked. The withering looks that Claire and Nicole delivered simultaneously made Robby scurry away to the back room.

Claire finished her work day at the shop an hour early in order to scope out something that had been picking at her while she tried to fall asleep after the police and Detective Fuller left the townhouse last night. In the afternoon heat, she walked to a Back Bay neighborhood, turned onto the street she was looking for, and climbed the stairs to a brownstone building and pressed a button on the intercom panel outside the glossy black door. As Claire admired the professional landscaping around the front of the building, the lock on the door buzzed and she was admitted to the tastefully decorated lobby where the doorman sat at a dark wood desk.

"I'm a friend of a tenant here and I haven't heard from her for days. Would the building manager be able to check her apartment for me?"

The man nodded and made a phone call and in a few minutes, a short, stocky woman dressed in slacks and a red blouse hurried down the hall, greeted Claire, and walked her away from the security desk to a sitting area in front of a fireplace.

"You're worried about your friend?" the older woman asked.

"I haven't heard from her for days. I don't know her relatives or other friends so I thought I'd come check with you. Her name is Merritt Handley."

The woman's face tensed and her gaze flitted about the lobby. "Ms. Handley told me that she doesn't have any relatives. She works all the time. You're the only person who has come to inquire about her, well, besides the police and some man who claimed to be her boyfriend." She rolled her eyes.

"The police were here?" Claire knew that they'd probably made a visit to Merritt's apartment since she'd shared her concerns with law enforcement, but she pretended to be surprised.

The woman touched Claire's arm reassuringly. "When I let the police into the apartment, nothing was wrong. Everything was in place. There was no sign of a struggle. The police suspected that Merritt just went off without telling anyone."

"Merritt's boyfriend came by?" Claire asked.

The woman's eyes darkened. "He wasn't her boyfriend. I'm sure of it. Ms. Handley wouldn't be interested in someone like him."

"Why do you say that?"

"He was dressed okay, but he looked like a thug. I never saw him with Ms. Handley. She's lived here for ages and I never saw him around here, not once. I'm here all the time, I would have noticed him."

Claire's heart thumped. "Have you seen Merritt lately?"

"I haven't, no. I'm worried about her, same as you." The woman glanced around and lowered her voice. "Just a few minutes ago, I ran into the people who live in the apartment next to Ms. Handley. They reported some noise coming from her apartment last night." The woman's lips were pinched together in two tight, thin lines. "I was going up there to take a look. I want the security guard to accompany me. Since you're here, you may come up with us, but you'll have to remain in the hallway while we go in."

"Okay." Claire nodded as a rush of anxiety flooded her veins.

The three took the elevator to the seventh floor where they entered a wide corridor with dark wood wainscoting beneath cream-colored walls and polished wood floors with a thick subtle-patterned carpet running down the center. The subdued lighting lent an elegant and refined air to the space.

The building manager stopped at the second door on the right and paused in front of it with the master key in her hand. The security guard stood behind the woman and nodded to Claire. "I'll ask you to stay here in the hall while we go in and check things out."

The woman knocked, and when no one responded, she turned the key and gingerly pushed the door open. "Hello?" When she saw what was inside, the woman gasped and placed her hand over her mouth. The security guard gripped the canister of pepper spray attached to his belt as he entered the apartment.

Claire's head spun when she peeked over the manager's shoulder. What was once a beautiful room was now in total disarray with furniture overturned, the contents of drawers dumped onto the floor, and clothing strewn about the place. "I'll call the police," the manager mumbled.

Claire stepped around the distraught woman and entered Merritt's apartment being careful not to touch anything. The place was a disaster. As Claire moved slowly about, she could sense the leftover fury pulsing on the air and had the distinct feeling that the mess was not the result of someone searching for something, but was the product of an unbridled fit of rage. Claire felt her throat constricting like there wasn't enough oxygen in the room and she turned abruptly and hurried out to the hallway.

"The police are coming. How did this happen?" The manager's eyes looked teary. "Ms. Handley probably wasn't at home when this happened. She must be fine. Don't you think so?"

Claire didn't answer the question. "Does Merritt have a car? Is her car in the parking garage?"

The manager's eyes widened. "A car? Yes, she does. She rents a space in the garage."

"What kind of a car is it?" Claire had a sinking feeling in her stomach.

The manager's face was pale. "I know what she drives because I have the same car, just a different color." She told Claire the make, model, and color of Merritt's vehicle and Claire dashed away. "I'm going down there. I want to see if her car is in the garage. If I'm not back when the police come, please send an officer down."

Claire punched at the elevator buttons, got in, and rode to the basement. Dizziness had taken over and she shook herself slightly to try to clear her head. Rushing up and down the parking lanes of the garage, she searched for a car that met the manager's description of Merritt's vehicle and when she was nearly through the space, some measure of relief passed over her. Only the far end of the garage was left and it looked to have just four cars parked there. None of them belonged to Merritt.

Turning to leave, something in the furthest corner caught Claire's eye and her heart dropped.

Merritt's car was pulled in behind a cement column.

Shuffling slowly to the corner, Claire's muscles began to tremble and as she stepped close to the car, she could see something dark puddled on the cement floor beneath the trunk.

Blood.

CHAPTER 26

When the police arrived and the car's trunk was opened, Merritt Handley's body was found inside. She had been strangled and stabbed. Claire, the building manager, and the security guard were questioned and allowed to leave. Detective Fuller arrived and asked Claire why she was at Merritt's building.

"I was worried about her. I thought I'd come by." Claire eyed Fuller. "I suppose there isn't any point in asking what you know?"

Fuller shoved his hands into his pockets. "I can't talk about an ongoing investigation."

"Do you know where Melody is?"

Fuller's face was blank, not giving anything away.

Still unsure about whether or not she could trust the detective, Claire had decided not to share anything with him that he did not specifically ask. "I'm going home now."

As she started away, Fuller called to her.

"Claire...."

When she looked back at him, he sighed and shrugged a shoulder.

Arriving home somber and pensive, Claire took the dogs for a walk and pondered Merritt Handley and what had caused her death. She was certain that Attorney Freeman was responsible for Merritt's death, either directly or by his order, but she wondered which side Merritt had been on. Was she working *with* Freeman or against him? The circumstances of Merritt's life picked at Claire.

The building manager had told Claire that Merritt didn't have a boyfriend, had no family, and never saw Merritt with any friends. The idea of the young woman spending her life alone, focused solely on working and building a career struck Claire as terribly sad and she thought about the parallels between her and Merritt's lives. Before she'd met Teddy, Claire had been single-minded about accumulating money as a buffer to the poverty she'd experienced while growing up. To her, money was security and stability and that was what Claire longed for.

That could have been me back there in that trunk. I was like Merritt. Working, working. Never taking time for friends or relationships. Alone. All alone. Claire brushed a tear from her eye and said a silent prayer of thanks for the good fortune of having met her husband. *Teddy saved me.*

An hour went by with Claire and the dogs strolling around the Common, the financial district, and down to the waterfront. Deciding she'd better return home, she made a loop through the city heading back to her neighborhood. Walking the dogs past a storefront with huge panes of glass, Claire caught her reflection in the window and pushing a lock of her hair behind her ear, she realized she hadn't had her hair cut for over a year.

For a split second, she thought of calling Alicia for an appointment to get her hair trimmed and her heart constricted when the reality hit her that the hairstylist was dead. Thinking how odd that such a trivial thing as a haircut would pop into her mind when she'd been thinking so seriously about Merritt and her own life, Claire stopped in her tracks and stared at her image in the glass, her head buzzing.

Alicia.

Claire was nearly overcome with the pressing need to talk to Alicia's husband again.

***

When Tony saw Claire enter his deli, his face scrunched with concern. "What's wrong with you?"

Claire sank into the café chair in the corner and proceeded to tell Tony about Merritt. "I feel like I need to talk to Alicia's husband again. I think there's a clue hiding there."

Tony rubbed his meaty hand over his forehead and shook his head slowly. "Stay away from it, Blondie. It's nothing but a viper pit. When people go looking for trouble, they usually find it."

"I've found plenty already."

Tony frowned. "Then my advice to you is to retire from investigative pursuits."

Claire ignored the comment. "Where could Melody be?"

"Maybe she met with the same fate."

"Please don't say that." Claire rested her chin in her hand. "Alicia, Siobhan, and Merritt are dead. It has to stop." Sipping from the cup of ice cold water Tony had brought her, Claire looked over at her friend. "What's going on with you? Is there any news about the building?"

"There seems to be a second offer." Tony let out a long, defeated sigh. "It's well over the asking price for the building. The owner is going to accept it."

Claire narrowed her eyes. "Do you know who the buyer is?"

Tony shook his head. "Some financial group."

"Maybe the buyer will let you stay." Claire gave Tony a hopeful look. "Maybe the new owner would be very glad to have a long-established tenant remain in the building."

Tony's face was serious. "I doubt it. A financial

group usually has one goal, to make money. Renting to me doesn't fit that objective."

The dogs whined and lay down under the table at Tony's feet.

"Give me your hand," Claire said, wanting to lighten the mood.

Tony leaned back in his chair and looked at Claire suspiciously. "Why?"

Reaching for the big man's hand, Claire smiled. "I'm going to tell your fortune."

"You're a fortune teller now?" Tony crossed his arms over his chest.

"Maybe." Claire chuckled. "How hard can it be? Give me your hand. Humor me."

Tony shook his head and placed his hand on the table, palm side up. Running her index finger over the lines in the man's palm, Claire peered at the calloused hand, muttering 'hmmm' and 'ahhh' until she glanced up with a serious expression. "Very interesting."

"What does your sixth sense tell you? That I own a deli?"

Claire smiled. "It does tell me that, yes, but there's more. You see this line here?" She pointed. "It tells me that you have a very long life ahead."

"Impoverished, I suppose."

Claire ignored him. "Look at these two lines. See how they criss-cross? Do you know what that means?"

Tony grumped. “That I have a nut pretending to read my palm?”

Claire couldn’t stifle her chuckle. “Never mock the fortune teller, kind sir.” Forcing a serious tone, she continued, “The criss-crossing lines mean that you are at a crossroads. Things will change.”

“I didn’t need a palm reading to figure that out.”

“But things will change for the better.” Claire’s eyes twinkled. “You will prosper. You will know stability. You will get what you wish for.”

“Maybe in my next life.” Tony stood up.

Claire stretched out her hand. “That will be twenty-five dollars for the reading, thank you very much.”

Tony walked to the deli counter and said over his shoulder, “Send me the bill.”

Claire pretended to frown. “Oh, I will. With interest.”

Claire’s phone buzzed with an incoming text and when she picked it up, the levity drained from her face. She read the caller’s name several times to be sure she wasn’t imagining the words.

It was from Alicia Fitchburg’s husband, Paul.

Can you come to the house? I need to talk to you.

CHAPTER 27

Claire left the Corgis with Tony, and against his advice, she headed off for Paul Fitchburg's home to find out what it was he needed to talk to her about. When he opened the front door, Paul looked like he'd aged ten years. His facial muscles sagged and his eyes were bloodshot. His appearance made Claire's heart race with anxiety.

She followed him into the house and when they were settled on the living room sofa, Paul leaned forward, his elbows on his knees, his head in his hands. "Now Merritt is dead." His voice shook.

"I didn't say anything to you about it because I wasn't sure if you'd heard the news. I'm sorry," Claire told him.

"She was so young. A life wasted." Paul didn't look up.

"How did you find out?"

"I have a buddy who works at the police station. He knew we were close with Merritt when she was young. He let me know." Paul cleared his throat.

"When you were here last, I left some things out of our conversation."

Claire leaned forward.

"I should have told you." Paul looked like he was about to cry. "Alicia didn't tell me everything. In light of what's happened, I think she was trying to protect me."

Sitting on the edge of her seat, Claire watched Paul with wide eyes waiting for him to tell her the details.

"I told you the truth that I didn't see Merritt much, but Alicia was seeing her quite a bit. Alicia was worried about something that Merritt confided to her. My wife was afraid that Merritt was mixed up in something she shouldn't have been. I didn't link Alicia's death to what Merritt was involved with, maybe because I've been in a fog since I lost my wife. I feel like I'm not thinking straight."

"Did Alicia tell you anything about what Merritt was doing?"

Paul shook his head. "She only said that it seemed dangerous and she was going to try and talk Merritt out of it."

"From the things Alicia *did* say to you, are you able to figure anything out? What was going on?"

"It seemed to have something to do with that law firm Merritt was working for. Maybe she was involved in some case that might have been dangerous? Whatever it was, I think it got Alicia killed." Paul rubbed at his eyes.

"Have you talked to the police about your concerns?"

"I haven't." Paul took a quick look across the room to a desk on the far wall.

"It might help with the investigation," Claire said.

"I don't know. I don't know if it would help."

Claire asked gently, "Why are you telling *me* about this?"

Paul bit his lower lip. "Because Merritt asked me to."

Claire almost slipped off the sofa to the floor. "Merritt? When? How?"

"In a letter." Paul walked to the desk and returned with a small package wrapped in brown paper with a letter folded and slipped under the string that was tied around it. "This arrived this morning." Paul removed the letter and handed it to Claire.

Dear Paul,

I'm sending you this package for safekeeping. If anything happens to me, please contact Claire Rollins and give the package to her. She will figure out what to do with it. I'm so very sorry about Alicia. You have always been good to me.

Love,

Merritt

Claire's cell phone number was printed at the bottom of the page.

When she handed the letter back to Paul, Claire's mouth was hanging open. Paul lifted the package from his lap and held it out to her. "You're supposed to take this."

Accepting it with trembling hands, Claire asked, "Did you look at it? Do you know what it is?"

Paul shook his head. "I'm not sure I want to know."

Claire had a pretty good idea what was inside. The package was about the size of a small book, about the size of the notebook Claire had seen Melody Booker hand to Merritt at the airport.

Lifting her eyes to Paul, she asked, "Do you know where Melody is?"

Paul's eyebrows shot up. "No. Absolutely not. I would tell you, if I knew." The man's chin dipped. "I suppose Melody is mixed up in the terrible trouble of this, too."

"I think she is." Claire's voice was soft. "I'd like to open the package and see what's inside. Are you okay with that?"

Paul swallowed and nodded, but he slid a couple of inches away from Claire.

When the brown paper was removed, the notebook that Melody had handed to Merritt was revealed inside. Claire opened the cover and flipped through some of the pages. Handwritten notes were written on every page. Turning to the beginning, Claire began to read. It was an extensive and detailed account of the harassment that Melody was subjected to working at Fast Freight. Dates, names, and actions had been carefully recorded. After reading for several minutes, Claire flipped to a section of the notebook that had a tab attached to one of the pages and scanned some of the entries. She read part of it aloud.

Merritt Handley got in touch with me today. We talked about what was going on at Fast Freight. She's heard things about an attorney who is a partner in a firm downtown. She knows him from court. She's heard some rumors and thinks he might be involved with a criminal ring working out of the airport. He's asked her to join his firm. She is going to accept to try and find out what he's up to.

Paul cleared his throat. "Merritt was a good person. She always wanted to do the right thing."

Claire read another entry.

Things seem to be escalating. We have to meet in private. Merritt knows that Alex Freeman is running something illegal at the airport. She thinks he's making millions of dollars, but doesn't have firm evidence. Yet. We think the guys who have been harassing me are working with Freeman.

The next section that Claire read caused her

heart to jump into her throat. She warned Paul about what was written and he nodded for Claire to go ahead and read it out loud.

Merritt is very upset. She's been confiding in Alicia Fitchburg about everything. Alicia kept telling Merritt to stop investigating, that it was too dangerous, but Merritt won't stop. She's determined to bring Alex Freeman to justice. Alicia went to the police and told them our suspicions about Freeman. Yesterday Alicia was found murdered. Someone at the police station has to be working with Freeman. The dirty cop must have told Freeman about Alicia's visit to the police station. We don't know if Alicia told our names to the police, but Merritt and I know that now we are in danger.

Paul wept with his hands covering his face. "Alicia was only trying to help. She thought the police would go after Freeman and that Merritt and Melody would be safe." Claire closed the notebook and moved closer to the man. She put her arm around his shoulders, her own tears running down her cheeks.

***

Claire stayed with Paul Fitchburg for another hour before leaving to pick up the dogs and head home. She and Paul decided that, for the time being, it would be safer for him to keep the notebook at his home and not to share it with law enforcement until Claire had spoken with Judge Augustus Gunther and found out who in the department could be trusted.

Tony had sent Claire a text to say he'd gone out to help a friend with a plumbing problem and to use the key code on his door to pick up the dogs. Walking up the hill to her townhouse with the Corgis on their leashes, Claire thought that the dogs were acting oddly, sniffing everywhere and letting out occasional growls and she suspected that they had picked up on her own uneasy emotional state. "It's okay, everything's okay," she told the dogs even though she knew they wouldn't believe a word of what she was saying.

Climbing the steps to the townhouse, Claire sighed audibly, her mind worn out and her body fatigued and sluggish. Dropping her keys on the entryway side table, she called for Nicole even though the apartment was dark. "Are you home?"

No one answered.

Claire dragged herself to the living room and not bothering to turn on the lights, she slid the door open so the dogs could go out into the garden. Bear had his nose to the floor sniffing all around the apartment, the hair standing up on his back. He stood at the open living room door sniffing the air and then darted into the yard with a growl. Lady moved to the door watching her dog friend. She stood like a statue for several moments, turned her head to the dining room, and then followed after Bear into the garden.

Watching the dogs, a shiver ran slowly down Claire's back. "We're all on edge," she muttered.

A note from Nicole was on the refrigerator. The fire alarm company called her to report that the alarm had gone off at the chocolate shop and she'd gone down there to see what was going on.

Claire kicked off her shoes and headed for her bedroom wanting to shower and change into pajamas. In the master bath, she was about to turn the shower knob to start the water when a noise in the living room caused her hand to freeze in mid-air. It sounded like the door to the garden was sliding shut.

Feeling like her body was flooding with ice water, Claire hurried to the wall switch and flicked off the lights. Her heart pounding, she tip-toed into the bedroom and turned the lights off in that room. The dogs growled and barked frantically on the other side of the living room door and Claire cursed herself for leaving her cell phone in the kitchen. She couldn't remain in the bedroom, she had to do something.

Peering carefully into the dark hallway, Claire moved her feet slowly and carefully trying not to make the wood floor squeak and she shuffled into the hall where she pressed her back against the wall and sucked in a deep breath. *Think, think.*

Claire considered trying to get to the front door, but if someone came at her, she had no weapon. If she could make it to the kitchen, she could get a knife and rush to the doors leading to the garden so that she and the dogs could fight the intruder together. She knew that neither choice was a good one.

Deciding to try for the kitchen, Claire's sense of hearing was on high alert noticing every little sound even with the din of the dogs barking outside. She hadn't turned a light on in the kitchen, but her eyes had adjusted to the darkness as she slid her feet quietly over the floor to the counter drawer that held the sharpest knives.

As Claire reached to open the drawer, she saw movement reflected in the glass door of the wall-mounted microwave.

It was a man ... standing several yards behind her.

CHAPTER 28

Claire wheeled around to see Alex Freeman on the other side of the kitchen island staring at her, the whites of his eyes bright in the darkness. "You." Even though her head was spinning with fear, Claire practically spit the words out of her mouth. "What are you doing in my house?"

The dogs were howling in the yard and Claire could hear their frantic clawing at the glass door. She took a step forward towards the island. "How did you get in here?" She did not want to show her fear to Freeman so she continued to babble. "Where were you hiding?"

"I invited myself in. I hope you don't mind. You have a nice basement."

Claire couldn't see a weapon in Freeman's hands, but in the dark she couldn't be sure. "I do mind. Why don't you see yourself out?"

Freeman chuckled.

Claire took a step to the wall intending to flick on the lights.

"Don't move." The hate in Freeman's voice chilled Claire.

"I'm going to turn on the lights."

"Stand still."

While Claire's eyes darted around looking to see if Freeman was alone in the house, she realized the dogs had gone quiet and her heart thudded, fearing one of Freeman's helpers had hurt them. "Did you bring one of your flunkies with you?"

"No. I didn't. The last losers I sent here failed the job and are now tucked away in police custody. Fools. I really hope they're able to keep their mouths shut because that's the only way they'll ever draw another breath."

Moonlight filtered in through the windows and lit up Freeman's face. Beads of sweat glistened over his forehead and Claire thought he looked crazed. Feeling lightheaded and afraid that she might pass out, Claire stuck her fingernails into her palms to try to focus her mind. "Where's Melody?"

Freeman's right eyebrow raised. "I'm sure you must know."

"Wrong." Claire tried to sound bold and confidant, not like the pathetic wimp she felt to be. She continued to babble. "Why did you kill Merritt?"

Freeman released a breath of air. "What a waste. Such an intelligent woman. She had such a bright future."

"You took her future from her."

"She took it from herself. The traitor betrayed me ... working with Melody," Freeman muttered and shook his head as he advanced several steps. "They shouldn't try to stop me," he sneered at Claire. "Where's Melody?"

Realizing that the only reason she was still alive was because Freeman thought she knew where Melody Booker was hiding, Claire tried to buy time to figure out what she could do. "What are you doing at the airport? How are you making your money?"

"Melody didn't tell you? I thought she'd figured it out."

Claire shook her head.

"Can't *you* figure it out?" Freeman smiled. "My guys access the airline's computer system to find out the weight of the incoming cargo. The logs don't list the contents of the cargo, but they do list the weight. Isn't that stupid? It's basically the same things being shipped all the time, but when the weight goes up, then we know that what we want is arriving."

"What's on the plane that you want?"

"When the cargo weighs more, we know that the post office is shipping something valuable to this area. They're shipping new credit cards. The return address on the boxes is always the same. From South Dakota. You wouldn't believe how many cards come in on one shipment. My guys go in to unload the cargo, they find the boxes with the credit cards, and they remove the individually addressed envelopes containing the cards. We sell most of them. We keep some to make purchases with and then we sell the things we buy. It's very, very profitable."

"The police help you?"

"A couple of them do." Freeman's grin was like a sneer. "We have to cover our bases, you know."

"Who in law enforcement helps you?"

"Enough of this." Freeman reached behind his back and when his hand came forward he held a knife.

Claire's throat was so tight she could barely breathe any air into her lungs. When Freeman had moved for the knife, she saw a gun was strapped to his hip. Her mind was spinning. *How am I going to get out of this? What can I do?*

"Where is Melody Booker?" Freeman took several steps closer to the kitchen island.

Claire, standing on the opposite side, held the man's eyes. When Freeman took advancing steps around the island towards Claire, she moved in the opposite direction so that they were beginning to walk in a circle.

"Answer my question," Freeman sneered. "You *will* talk eventually."

"Why do you think I know where she is?"

"You seem to know a lot of things, things that are none of your business."

Claire tried to act tough. "I made it my business after your flunkies' bullets got too close to us."

"Not close enough, it seems. But don't worry. *My* bullet won't miss."

"It won't matter. You'll be arrested soon. We have Melody's notebook. She wrote everything down in it."

Freeman's eyes bore into Claire's. "That notebook isn't proof of anything."

Moving her arm slowly, Claire edged her fingers to the knob of one of the kitchen cabinet drawers and gently slid it open just enough to reach inside. "It will help though, once they have your secret laptop."

Claire could see the man's chest rising and falling as his eyes bugged.

"What are you saying?" His voice was a hoarse whisper. "What do you know?"

Gripping the thing in her hand and removing it from the drawer, Claire said, "I know you keep that laptop in the safe in your office closet." She let the words sink in and then leaned forward. "They'll come with a search warrant ... and all your secrets won't be secret anymore."

Freeman looked wild. He dropped the knife and yanked the gun from its holster. As he brought up his arm, Claire extended hers and her finger pressed on the top of the canister releasing a shot of pepper spray right into Freeman's face. He let out a cry of surprise and as Claire dropped to the floor, a thundering boom rocked the walls of the house. The living room's glass doors shattered into a million pieces from the bullets of Detective Ian Fuller's gun and two of them lodged in Alex Freeman's shoulder, bringing him down with a thud.

CHAPTER 29

Although Claire didn't know whose feet crunched over the shattered glass, she knew it was one of the good guys. When she heard others running into the house, she pushed herself to sitting position. The kitchen lights came on and in the dining room, a man's voice called out, *Clear!* just as Detective Fuller came around the island and peered down at Claire with worried eyes.

He knelt beside her and touched her shoulder. "Are you okay?"

Giving a shaky nod, Claire looked into his eyes. "I didn't trust you, you know. I thought you might be working with Freeman."

"I know. But I'm not." One side of Fuller's mouth turned up.

"I bet a lot of people don't trust you," Claire kidded him.

Fuller smiled as he helped Claire to her feet. "I'll have to work on that."

Officers had tended to Freeman's bloody

shoulder and Claire's face clouded as he was put on a stretcher by emergency personnel and taken out of the townhouse, moaning and wailing over his injury.

Claire felt no sympathy for the monster who was responsible for so much misery.

"How did you know? How did you know Freeman was here?"

Fuller said, "We didn't know it was Freeman who was here, we only suspected." He paused as a huge grin brightened his face. "You can thank two fine Corgis for alerting us."

Claire's eyebrows shot up.

"The dogs were outside a deli-market just a few blocks down the hill from here carrying on like it was the end of the world. The guy in the building called '911' and asked the dispatcher to send help to you. He also asked them to notify me." Fuller eyed Claire. "I understand a call came in from a former judge, as well. You have friends in high places, Ms. Rollins."

"Claire! Claire!" A familiar voice shouted and the woofs of dogs rang out from the open front door where several officers stood blocking the entrance.

"Let them through," called Fuller.

Tony rushed in behind the running Corgis and when he spotted Claire, his face looked like melting candle wax as he grabbed her in a hug and crumbled into tears of relief. The dogs leapt and danced and barked with joy around them and Claire bent to hug her *rescue* dogs, the word now having more than one meaning.

***

Alex Freeman, his law partner, Elan Johnson, two high-level police officers, and a dozen other men, some from Fast Freight, were arrested and charged with so many counts of wrongdoing that it boggled the mind. The secret laptop in Freeman's closet held thousands of words of incriminating evidence and when Claire was asked how she knew the laptop was there, she fibbed and told law enforcement she had seen him hiding it when she arrived for an appointment. When Detective Fuller heard her explanation, he eyed Claire with a raised eyebrow, but didn't ask her anything more.

When Melody Booker heard the news that Freeman has been arrested, she emerged from hiding in a friend's beach cottage that had been closed up for the season. Melody and Merritt had been working together to bring down Alex Freeman and his secret operation and they had been hiding together at the beach.

On the day when Merritt went back to her apartment, the young women decided to mail Melody's notebook to Alicia's husband for safekeeping. Because they couldn't access money from ATM machines or use credit cards in case their accounts were being monitored, Merritt, knowing the risks of returning to her building and ignoring Melody's pleas not to leave, made the decision to go home to retrieve some cash she had there. Freeman had a man watching the building. The man made his move when Merritt drove into the garage.

***

Claire, the dogs, Augustus Gunther, and Nicole clustered around a tiny table on the sidewalk outside of Tony's deli enjoying the sunshine and the lovely breeze that was chasing the humidity out of the city. Tony came outside carrying a tray of cold drinks for his friends. A bowl of water for the Corgis, and any other dogs that happened by, already sat on the sidewalk near the entrance to the store.

"I'd like to make a toast," Tony said, "to my friends and to my store. Tomorrow I'll be hosting an all-day buffet for my friends and customers who have supported me for so many years. I leave with a heavy heart." Tony cleared his throat. "But I am truly thankful for the more than fifty years I've been able to work here."

The building had been sold and Tony was closing the deli at the end of the week. The burly man raised his glass of ginger ale and the others joined him in lifting their glasses just as a man, well-dressed in a dark grey suit carrying a briefcase, walked up and spoke.

"Excuse me. Tony Martinelli?"

Tony turned to the man with a serious expression. "That's me."

"I represent the McGready Group, a financial institution here in Boston." The man removed a leather folder from his briefcase and handed it to Tony. "Congratulations, Mr. Martinelli."

Tony looked at the folder in his hand. "Did I win something?"

The man chuckled. "You might say so."

Tony appeared dumbfounded and the man explained. "Mr. Martinelli, an anonymous person has purchased this building." He gestured to the brick structure which housed Tony's deli and his apartment. "On your behalf."

Tony stood there with a blank face.

"Do you understand, Mr. Martinelli? This building belongs to you now. You are the owner."

Tony's mouth dropped open. "Me? How? Who?"

"Anonymous, Sir." The man pointed to the folder in Tony's hand. "The papers inside hold a copy of the deed and some other financial information. The name of the attorney who will be assisting you is also inside. Please contact him to set up an appointment for your signature and to go over the details. Congratulations, again." The man nodded to Tony and to the small group sitting around the table and then he strode away.

Tony turned to his friends, flabbergasted. "What just happened?"

Lady and Bear wagged their tails and let out happy barks.

Claire and Nicole hooted with joy and jumped up to give Tony a hug while Augustus beamed at them from his seat. When Claire glanced over at Augustus, the older man raised an eyebrow at her, and she only smiled and shrugged.

"Anonymous?" Tony sputtered. "Who would do such a thing for me? Who has the money to do such a thing?"

"Maybe the neighborhood got together and raised the money?" Nicole speculated.

"You have many wealthy customers," Claire said. "Someone just gave you the gift of a lifetime."

Tony looked at Augustus. "Is this above-board? Can a person gift a building to someone?"

"A person most certainly can." Augustus smiled broadly. "And someone just did."

Tony made eye contact with each of his friends. "Who could it be?"

Claire laughed. "Unknown, but you better be extra nice to everyone who walks in that door, just in case that is the person who did this for you."

"You will have to turn your going-away party tomorrow into an I'm-staying celebration." Augustus raised his glass and made a toast. "To places filled with good friends and good fortune. Congratulations to you, my friend. You are well-loved."

When what just happened finally hit him and he realized that he would never have to leave his store or home, tears of joy rolled down Tony's wrinkled cheeks. His friends teased him good-naturedly and as they made guesses about who might have arranged the unbelievable gift to Tony, someone walked up and joined the group.

"Celebrating?" Detective Fuller asked with a smile.

Everyone's face turned serious when they saw the law enforcement officer.

"Is something wrong?" Claire asked with worry tinging her words.

"Everything's good. I just went by your townhouse and no one answered my knock so I thought you might be here. What's going on?"

Tony explained the fabulous news that someone he knew had anonymously purchased the building for him.

Fuller congratulated Tony and then laughed. "I wish *I* knew your friends."

Pulling up a chair, Fuller joined the group and the conversation was pleasant and light. While he scratched both dogs' ears, Fuller turned to Claire. "You mentioned a while ago that you were training for a triathlon. I imagine you haven't had much time for exercise lately. I'm feeling a little out of shape and I feel like I need a goal. Getting ready for a triathlon would fit the bill. Would you mind a training buddy?"

Claire looked into Fuller's dark brown eyes. The terrible events of the past few weeks had made her suspicious and wary of the man and she was happy that her concerns about him had been completely false. She sensed that Fuller was smart and kind and loyal, and she wanted to have him in her life ... as a training partner, a friend, or maybe someday, something more.

With a warm smile, she held her hand out to the detective and they shook with one another. "I wouldn't mind at all. It would be great to have a training buddy."

The dogs woofed their agreement as warm little sparks danced along Claire's arm from the touch of Ian's hand holding hers.

THANK YOU FOR READING!

Author's Note:

If you'd like to know the information that influenced the idea for the crime in this story, please do an internet search on: Susan Taraskiewicz.

May her killer be brought to justice and may her family find peace.

***

BOOKS BY J.A. WHITING CAN BE FOUND HERE:
www.amazon.com/author/jawhiting

To hear about new books and book sales, please sign up for my mailing list at:
www.jawhitingbooks.com

Your email will never be sold, shared, or spammed.

BOOKS BY J. A. WHITING

CLAIRE ROLLINS COZY MYSTERIES:

Good Fortunes (A Claire Rollins Cozy Mystery Book 1)

A Claire Rollins Cozy Mystery Book 2 - Coming

LIN COFFIN COZY MYSTERIES

A Haunted Murder (A Lin Coffin Cozy Mystery Book 1)

A Haunted Disappearance (A Lin Coffin Cozy Mystery Book 2)

The Haunted Bones (A Lin Coffin Cozy Mystery Book 3)

A Haunted Theft (A Lin Coffin Cozy Mystery Book 4)

A Haunted Invitation (A Lin Coffin Cozy Mystery Book 5)

The Haunted Lighthouse (A Lin Coffin Cozy Mystery Book 6) - soon

The Haunted Valentine (A Lin Coffin Cozy Mystery Book 7) – Feb-Mar 2017

And more!

SWEET COVE COZY MYSTERIES

The Sweet Dreams Bake Shop (Sweet Cove Cozy Mystery Book 1)
Murder So Sweet (Sweet Cove Cozy Mystery Book 2)
Sweet Secrets (Sweet Cove Cozy Mystery Book 3)
Sweet Deceit (Sweet Cove Cozy Mystery Book 4)
Sweetness and Light (Sweet Cove Cozy Mystery Book 5)
Home Sweet Home (Sweet Cove Cozy Mystery Book 6)
Sweet Fire and Stone (Sweet Cove Cozy Mystery Book 7)
Sweet Friend of Mine (Sweet Cove Cozy Mystery Book 8)
Sweet Hide and Seek (Sweet Cove Cozy Mystery Book 9)
And more!

OLIVIA MILLER MYSTERIES

The Killings (Olivia Miller Mystery Book 1)
Red Julie (Olivia Miller Mystery Book 2)
The Stone of Sadness (Olivia Miller Mystery Book 3)

If you enjoyed the book, please consider leaving a review.

A few words are all that's needed.

It would be very much appreciated.

ABOUT THE AUTHOR

J.A. Whiting lives with her family in New England. Whiting loves reading and writing mystery stories.

VISIT ME AT:

www.jawhitingbooks.com

www.facebook.com/jawhitingauthor

www.amazon.com/author/jawhiting